Elza: The Girl

D1509641

Elza: The Girl

Sérgio Rodrigues

Translated by Zoë Perry

amazoncrossing 🄫

Boca Raton Public Library

This is a work of fiction. Names, characters, organizations, places, events, and incidents are either products of the author's imagination or are used fictitiously.

Text copyright © 2008 by Sérgio Rodrigues.
Translation copyright © 2014 by Zoë Perry.
All rights reserved.

No part of this book may be reproduced, or stored in a retrieval system, or transmitted in any form or by any means, electronic, mechanical, photocopying, recording or otherwise without express written permission of the publisher.

Previously published as *Elza: A Garota* by Editora Nova Fronteira in Brazil, 2008. Translated from Brazilian Portuguese by Zoë Perry. First published in English by AmazonCrossing in 2014.

Published by AmazonCrossing, Seattle
www.apub.com

Amazon, the Amazon logo, and AmazonCrossing are trademarks of Amazon.com, Inc. or its affiliates.

ISBN-13: 9781477819784
ISBN-10: 1477819789
Library of Congress Control Number: 2013919791

Cover design by David Drummond

Printed in the United States of America

For Daniel and Clarissa, my children.

"No atonement for God, or novelists, even if they are atheists. It was always an impossible task, and that was precisely the point. The attempt was all."

—Ian McEwan, *Atonement*

1

She was sixteen years old. Or so they say. The versions of the story vary. In some, Elza is a grown woman, twenty-one. In most, she's sixteen. While her age perhaps alters the union's degree of scandal, it does not change the fact that in 1935 Elza was the girlfriend, wife, companion, concubine, lover, and mistress of the secretary-general of the Brazilian Communist Party, the organization's highest rank. This was the same year that the Brazilian left attempted its most daring move and suffered its greatest defeat. Miranda was almost thirty. Personable, friendly, he told all the comrades that he loved Elza and intended as soon as political circumstances permitted to make an honest woman of her. But first he had to attend to the little job of seizing power in Brazil.

Elza Fernandes was more of a kid, even though at five feet two she stood as tall as the average Brazilian woman of that era. She might still have been growing. The coroners who examined her bones pinned her at sixteen, reporting a body still developing. Her exact age is one of the mysteries of this incomplete character. In our history, she wasn't even entitled to a definitive size, oscillating between young lady and adult. This is one of the more blatant errors among the many from case number 1381 of the National Security Tribunal, which in November 1940 sentenced Luís Carlos Prestes and six others to thirty-year prison sentences for the death of Elvira

Cupello Calônio, which occurred on March 1, 1936 (or perhaps shortly before or shortly after), sentences that all would be shortened by the amnesty for political prisoners decreed by the Brazilian president in 1945.

On one point, blind as it might be, Brazilian administrative zeal leaves no doubt: in April of 1940 judicial proceedings began to investigate the perpetrators of Elza's murder. According to the records, she was born in Sorocaba in 1914, daughter of Francisco Cupello Calônio and Emilia Luiza. The problem is that in the rest of the stacks of documents, in statement after statement, over months and months, there are references to Elza being sixteen, to Elza being a minor, to Elza's childish body, and that is that. Even the coroner's findings, the bone analysis, point decisively to an adolescent, but at no point did the proceeding seek to clarify the inconsistency that ran through it like a spear: How old was the deceased?

Prof. Marly Vianna, a former officer of the Brazilian Communist Party and one of the Brazilian academics who has devoted the most time and energy to the study of the events of 1935, told me, in her Rio living room filled with books, that she was convinced Elza's age had been lowered by the police, the press, and even the coroner in order to make the crime more heinous in the eyes of public opinion, which was already solidly opposed to the communists since the group's failed November insurrection. It was an invention correlated to the "communists eat children" cliché. The girl's young age would do the job of retouching an already ugly picture with paints shaded with cowardice. In other words, Elza actually was twenty-one. The right fabricated the idea that she was sixteen.

I replied that this wasn't quite true. Miranda had also said Elza was sixteen. Sara Becker, a communist militant from São Paulo, who on the eve of the insurrection of '35 was sent to Rio, met the girlfriend of the party's secretary-general at Rosa Meirelles's home, one of the informal bases of the conspiracy. This is also where Elza *used to go every afternoon to scrounge for some coffee and bread. Sara was eighteen at the time and described Elza to me as a young woman around the same age as her. She was adamant about this: the same age. If that doesn't prove she was sixteen, it does even less to prove that she was twenty-one. Then there's that damned skeleton, which the coroner had said was still growing. Was he bought by the government? True, it wouldn't have cost much to buy him off. But why? In the eyes of the courts—and in a "show trial" in which very strict defense conditions were offered to the accused—it wouldn't be necessary to find any legally aggravating circumstance, much less fabricate one. No particular age would make the homicide more of a homicide. To such a degree that until the very end, the official claim remained that the victim was born in 1914. If they were going to lie about her age, why wouldn't they do it right and falsify her date of birth on the court documents?*

The deeper you delve into the subject, the less likely the theory of her being twenty-one becomes. It is easier to imagine a typo, "1919" becoming "1914" through the fault of the registrar's bad handwriting or an illiterate or drunk father—or both—who got mixed up when the record was drawn up years after her birth. Or maybe the confusion was triggered by one of those professional lies the communists always had up their sleeves to confuse the repression, an array of fake names, fake ages, fake stories. Elza, born in the state of São Paulo, is referred to here and there as being born in Minas Gerais. In January 1936, when she was arrested, along with Miranda, in the apartment on Avenida Paulo de Frontin in Rio de Janeiro where the two were neighbors of a "public communist" such as writer Jorge Amado, Elza's crazy story became another one entirely. In her first statement, she told the police she didn't know her boyfriend's name or even her father's name. As to where she came from, on that she was unwavering: she said she had come from São Paulo. On foot.

They even say she was blond, but that might have been just another guise.

In this story, Elza will be sixteen years old, because one day Nilton Salles and Rubem Pereira de Araújo, investigators from the Rio de Janeiro Institute of Forensic Medicine, after examining the bones exhumed in a suburban backyard, wrote the following:

The ossification nuclei and the cartilage provided in the skeleton examined are commonly observed in women fifteen to sixteen years of age. Furthermore, we observed four intact wisdom teeth . . . Her age at the time of death must have been sixteen years.

Unfortunately, my searches at the two records offices in the city of Sorocaba failed to establish beyond all doubt Elvira Cupello Calônio's age. Hopefully, someone can fill in the blanks with what I wasn't able to discover. There were many things I wasn't able to discover, but this was the first one:

Elza's exact age when, deemed a traitor by the heads of the Brazilian Communist Party, she was strangled by the comrades with a clothesline and buried inside a burlap sack in the backyard of a deserted house in Guadalupe.

How old she'll be forever.

Molina had just turned forty-three and was looking for a story worth telling when he found Xerxes, or rather when Xerxes found him. His mind-set, neighboring on boredom and fatigue, was that there were no stories left in the world that would outweigh the work of telling them, whether through words, pictures, gestures, dance, smoke signals, telepathy, or any other means. That feeling began to change one April afternoon when he stepped into the old man's apartment, a cramped two-bedroom in Flamengo, for the first time. He had answered a classified ad. A few days later, nothing remained of his belief that there were no important stories left to tell. He could barely handle dividing his days between reading old newspapers, conversations with Xerxes in his living room cluttered with books, and feverish hours spent at his computer, banging out pages and pages that Molina knew beyond a doubt *needed* to be written. At the time, it hadn't occurred to him that maybe the story wasn't ready to be read yet.

Xerxes—Molina decided to just call him that, for reasons similar to those that made a girl who had been baptized Elvira become known as Elza—gave him more than just a great story. When the two first met, Molina had been unemployed and immersed in misanthropic seclusion that only Camila, his girlfriend, twenty years his junior, could break. Stories so tiny, so petty, besieged Molina, confining the world to a stupid present without origin or consequence. Thinking back to those days later on, he realized it was as if Xerxes were more than his source or a storyteller: he was History incarnate. Perhaps it's understandable that in such a state of mind Molina had failed to take into account the signs that not everything was as it seemed.

Xerxes said, "The less there is at stake, the greater the violence of the litigants. Make two hungry men compete over a slice of bread with some lard, and the battle will be grisly, maybe deadly. Leave two cigar-chomping capitalists to argue about, between sips of cognac, who will drag over to his side of the contract that percentile crumb representing millions, there you'll have a beautiful climate of civility presiding over the table!"

The first thing that caught Molina's attention was that the old man spoke as if he were writing, commas and all. Such power of articulation was something from another time, and it was only then that the nearly impossible age of the man—ninety-four, according to the newspaper—came crashing down in the living room before him like a boulder, a totem pole, a pyramid.

"Hypocritical civility," Xerxes continued, "isn't discussed, but it is still preferable to a stab in the artery. It follows that in a class society, peaceful coexistence is a bourgeois luxury."

Molina had arrived riled up and exasperated, having just scratched Camila's car on a pole, trying to park in a ridiculously tight spot, and then seeing two rogue parking attendants vying over the right to charge him for the privilege of parking there. The feeling of impending apocalypse that hung over the city, with its eternal present flattened behind and in front like a compact car squeezed into a parking spot for a tricycle—that familiar buzz hadn't come through the door with him. It was another time in that shadowy living room covered in books and black-and-white photographs in heavy frames. Molina had the presence of mind to tell the old man that his thinking was charming but it ignored centuries of empires founded on crime. "All members of the elite are violent," he pontificated. He was surprised by his own voice.

"I thought I was the communist," Xerxes said, smiling as he sat bolt upright in his armchair. He drummed his fingers on the handle of his cane resting on the floor between his pasty, scrawny legs, sprouting out from his baggy shorts. It was an abnormally muggy day for early October, but Xerxes's long and bony body was wrapped in a gray cardigan over a white T-shirt, thick tartan socks and leather sandals on his long feet. "The violence of the elite," he said, "is something I know well." His little eyes, the same color green as dirty water, fixed on Molina's eyes. "But that's another story. You're the one who came here telling me about the automobile minders who almost killed themselves over the crumbs that fall from the table of the petty bourgeoisie—that is, from *your* table."

"And what are you, sir? A worker?" When Molina said this, it felt aggressive even though that wasn't his intention. He was trying to lighten the mood, kid around with the old man. Maybe keep him from noticing how out of place he felt in this living room on the edge of time.

"I am a revolutionary intellectual," Xerxes said. "That's what I would have replied a long time ago. A petty bourgeois who, through reflection, disciplined reading of Leninist theory, and political and union work, was able to overcome the pathetic limitations of his class and rise to a higher consciousness, where the inexorability of history shines forth. Maria!" he shouted all of a sudden. They waited in silence until the maid, who also was elderly, came out from the kitchen. "Coffee," he ordered, then looping back. "But that was a long time ago. Today I'm just an old communist. You can call me a petty bourgeois, I don't care. I've been called so many things: Zinovievist, Trotskyist, leftist, rightist, opportunist. What are you, a journalist?"

Molina said he was. It was simpler and less dangerous than declaring himself a writer. Someone who declares himself a writer always runs the risk of hearing the question "Ah, and what have you written?" Embarrassing if you had never written anything. Anyway, the ad in the paper hadn't mentioned the word "writer." Xerxes was looking, in his curious phrasing, for "an editor-journalist-scriptwriter with a love of history and patience for the infirmities of an old, defeated revolutionary to help him write his memoirs."

At Xerxes's urging, Molina gave an overview of his career, trying probably unsuccessfully to mask the signs of decline that proliferated as the chronological order moved from the roles of editor to contributor, and the outlets from major newspapers to suspect periodicals. The old man listened to everything with attention. Feeling his presentation was lacking pizzazz, Molina thought about adding that he was one of the world's foremost experts on history's greatest television series, *The Twilight Zone.* He backed down in time, realizing it was unlikely that would earn him any points with Xerxes. He concluded by enumerating his elusive accomplishments and explained that now everything had changed. He was independent, he wouldn't be working under any more bosses, and he was investing in a slower, less superficial journalism only possible in books. That's why, when he'd read the classified ad, he thought it was a good fit for him. He prattled on abjectly from pure nervousness. The old man's silence disconcerted him. Totem, sphinx. As if it contained a silent but ruthless judgment of that hollow present, made before the court of a more authentic time, both in misery and in glory. Molina could only imagine the volume of Xerxes's memoirs, and all of a sudden the idea of the work that awaited him seemed terrifying.

If, of course, he took the job. But he had to take the job, didn't he? It was already his. A book. Guaranteed monthly income for three months, the old man explained, maybe more. Nothing as luxurious as his current unemployed status made it seem under the circumstances, but certainly decent. He later discovered that the money was Xerxes's own; there was no publisher, NGO, or foundation mixed up in documenting the memoir of a communist Methuselah. You could hear the muffled groans of the buses braking below at the stoplight nearly opposite the cinema, where years earlier a more misguided generation of Rio residents were convinced that Jean-Luc Godard was going to change the history of mankind.

"What do you know," asked Xerxes, "about the insurrection of 1935?"

"The Intentona?"

Xerxes nodded.

"Well, what everyone . . ."

"Wrong answer, son. What everyone knows about that is zip, zilch. No one knows anything about anything anymore, that's true, but they know even less about the Intentona. Ask the college students," said the old man with a wry grin to emphasize that he was alluding to the television quiz show, the one where the contestants could pass on some of the questions they couldn't answer to a panel of college students. "College students, for the most part, don't know either. Ask the college students, even the history majors, and they'll barely be able to tell you the difference between the Coluna Prestes social rebel movement and the military uprising of '35. How much you wanna bet?"

"I know a history major who does know," Molina was going to reply, but the old man's choice of words threw him off. "Military uprising?"

"Yes, are you surprised? There's no better term to define what happened in '35. The fragility of the attempt, the grotesque errors of political judgment committed by the conspirators, as well as the ferocious repression that ensued, with consequences that would influence the direction of the country for decades. In the book of Latin American uprisings, that, with its tragicomic flavor, is one of the most remarkable chapters. A pretty big book actually."

"A real brick," Molina agreed. "Nevertheless," he amended to his surprise, since he didn't know all that much about the matter—maybe he was trying to flatter the old communist—"in spite of all that, it was a fascinating venture."

"Fascinating venture, *my arse*," Xerxes snapped back, his caricatural European accent softening the curse. "That was just stupid, son. It set this country's political maturity back half a century, a disgrace. Fascinating venture."

"Of course there were errors of judgment," Molina said, not understanding why he was being so stubborn. "Serious errors yes, but the courage of those men . . ."

"What does courage have to do with it? Courage is all well and good, but misused it amounts to less than the salary of Maria here." Xerxes took from the hands of the servant, who had just entered the room, the stainless tray with the white cups and ceramic sugar bowl. With supernatural aplomb for someone his age, his cane leaning to the side against the arm of the chair, he gently laid the whole thing, which looked heavy, on the coffee table. "Sugar? Two spoonfuls?" He served Molina with trembling hands. Then he squeezed eight drops of sweetener into his own cup.

"Do you know the difference between a son of a bitch on the extreme right and a son of a bitch on the extreme left?" Xerxes asked, stirring his coffee. "The son of a bitch on the extreme right knows he's a son of a bitch."

"The one on the extreme left doesn't know?"

"No, he hasn't got a clue. He thinks he's purer than Saint Francis of Assisi." Xerxes guffawed, took a sip from his cup, and burst into a coughing fit so intense he almost spilled his coffee.

They were alone in the room again—Maria had disappeared somewhere inside the apartment. Molina took the cup from Xerxes's hands and offered to get some water, but the old man waved that he didn't need it. He gradually regained his composure and caught his breath. Soon he was pulling himself to his feet with a soft groan, supported by his cane. "There's a book I wanted to show you," he said, motioning for Molina to follow him.

On the shelves lining the walls, framed black-and-white photographs occupied the few spaces not filled by books: men dressed in suits, and women in buttoned-up dresses. Art books, books on history, mostly communist, with spines of every color. The old man walked slowly. Molina followed him.

The bedroom also had a lot of books, but fewer than the living room. Only one of the walls was covered in shelves. It didn't take long for Xerxes to find what he was looking for, a copy of E. M. Forster in English. After quickly leafing through it, he held out the open volume to Molina, who read the words underlined in pencil while listening to the old man recite with an unbearably posh accent, "'If I had to choose between betraying my country and betraying my friend, I should hope I have the guts to betray my country.' Do you agree?"

Was this a language test?

"Let me see. 'If I had to choose between betraying my country and betraying my friend . . .'"

"'. . . I should hope I have the guts to betray my country.' Do you agree?"

A test of morals for sure. And political ideology.

"It depends on what he means by country," Molina said, trying to buy some time, "and it depends on the friend."

"Typical answer from a young person," the old man scoffed.

"I'm not young."

"You are to me. You're a boy."

Xerxes sank back onto the narrow bed and invited Molina to sit on a dusty little ottoman next to the door. In another corner of the room, next to the dark wardrobe that looked to be a hundred years old, was a folding bamboo screen.

Xerxes said, "Prestes did what Forster was recommending, even though he probably never read it. He stuck with his friend, the Communist Party, and betrayed his country. Do you agree with this?"

"Of course not," Molina said, shaking his head.

"Why not?"

"Prestes made a lot of mistakes, but he was a patriot. He didn't betray his country."

"But he came over to Brazil with his foreign buddies to lead a plot funded by the Comintern, did he not?"

Was Xerxes being serious? Or was he not a communist at all? What was this old guy up to anyway?

"That," Molina replied, "was the basis for President Vargas's anticommunist propaganda."

The old man smiled, seemingly happy.

"Right answer. And not just Vargas. Until the end of the military dictatorship, in the '80s, when I was already an old man, right-wing discourse was just an extension of what it had been in 1935. The anticommunism that dominated twentieth-century Brazilian society was born with Vargas. It matured and grew old from 1964 onward with the generals, but the source of it all, the hub, could be found in the 1930s. If you look carefully, you'll find that the heart of the heart of our nitwit anticommunism is something tremendous that occurred in 1935: Prestes fell. The hero toppled."

In the brief silence that followed, Molina distinctly felt the air growing heavy, laden with grief.

"For millions of people in this country," Xerxes continued, a new fervor in his voice, "Prestes died as a political leader when he came to take over Brazil with the help of a foreign power, accompanied by agents of a foreign power in the pay of a foreign power. That was what Getúlio Vargas's police spread and the press gleefully reiterated in infinite variations with great care. The problem is that this wasn't a lie. Of course Prestes didn't come to take power *for* Moscow; he came to take power for himself. It is also absurd to think that the goal of '35 was to install in Brazil, right off the bat, a dictatorship of the proletariat, albeit the suntanned version of a semicolonial country. Nothing like that. We weren't that crazy. Prestes's government would be a compromise, the feasible government, or nothing at all. But were the Russians footing the bill for the revelry, with the leadership of the plot on the payroll? Indeed they were. If you have an advanced, international view of the world, there is nothing more to it. Countries are fictions, historical constructions destined to become obsolete in a classless society. Prestes's homeland, like mine, was the proletariat. But try convincing Joe Shmoe. The number of Brazilians who never forgave Prestes is inestimable. And lamentable."

Molina shifted on the ottoman, more confused than ever. "Sir, you're speaking as if you haven't forgiven Prestes either."

The old man stared at him for a few moments. "You can't imagine who Luís Carlos Prestes was in this country from 1925 to 1935, between the Coluna social rebel movement and the military uprising."

Molina replied that he knew Prestes was a great man.

Xerxes said, "Great? The greatest native son, my boy. A myth of extraordinary force, respected in the military like no other, and loved by the people far and wide. A monster in mystique, a genius in campaign maneuvers. But a disaster in politics; at least the kind of politics done in political offices."

"If you don't mind me saying so, sir, you have a funny way of expressing yourself for a communist."

"You think that because you are young and naïve. I am as communist as anyone. But I think with my head."

"Which for a long time was a hell of a contradiction."

"That's true," he laughed. "An oxymoron. I'm past that age now."

"Aren't we all? Isn't the world?"

The old man stood up on his cane, walked slowly to the folding screen, and disappeared behind it. Molina was surprised to realize after a few moments that he was changing his clothes.

"Son, I want you to read everything you can find about this key moment in your country's history," said Xerxes, his head bobbing above the bamboo screen. "I don't have time to sit here explaining the basics to you every couple of minutes. The story is going to have to come out all at once. As you can see, my time is short."

"I can hardly wait to start," Molina replied in a tone that struck him as sounding, sadly, like bootlicking.

Xerxes emerged from behind the screen wearing a ter-rycloth robe that had once been bright yellow. Tall, fragile, hunched over, he made Molina think of a battered and fried piece of asparagus. He walked to the nightstand next to the bed, opened the top drawer, and took out a fat manila envelope. On his way to the master bathroom, he handed it to Molina.

"For you to have some fun with. Read it all, but pay special attention to one name: Elza Fernandes. Come back tomorrow at the same time, and don't forget to bring a tape recorder and tapes, lots of tapes. I'm going to take a bath. On your way out, ask Maria to come help me. So long," he said, and shut the door in Molina's face.

2

Elza, a blond? The O Globo *newspaper reporter swore she was. Whether we can trust the reporter is a different story. All we have to go on is his article from the January 16, 1936 issue about the arrests of Adalberto (another of Miranda's aliases) and Elza. According to the article, an agent from the Department of Social Order arrived at 606 Paulo de Frontin Avenue, a luxury apartment building, and proceeded to unit 11, which was believed to be the headquarters of extremist conspirators. A blond-haired, blue-eyed young woman answered the door. When the agent from the Department of Social Order inquired about Adalberto, the young woman replied that he did not live there, and she further insisted as such upon subsequent questioning by the agent, who later reported to have been disarmed by the young woman's remarkable charm, though he did not fail to arrest her.*

The report was written in a kitschy style typical of the coverage given the Elza Fernandes case. Journalism in those days had already started leaning toward genre fiction, but after the uprising the news resorted to manipulating the reader's baser instincts in even larger doses—in this case, serving a clear political agenda. Mood was worth more than facts; dramatic effect drowned out exactness. In this atmosphere some blatant lies were able to flourish about the 1935 uprising, a movement that, after being stanched by the military in a matter of hours, would spend the following decades being clobbered on the field of propaganda, as if lacking in actual flaws. The strongest of these lies, reiterated for years every November in the agenda issued by the military commanders, and that the 1964 dictatorship forced the press to publish, was the one about hordes of loyalist military officers being stabbed to death by insurgents while they slept, in a stunning display of cowardice. Even though proven wrong by a heavyweight "bourgeois" historian, Hélio Silva, this legend still finds unsuspecting believers among us to this day.

Therefore, better to never exclude the possibility it's a bunch of baloney. One cannot rule out that Elza may have turned blond merely for the screenwriter's convenience, since it was the hair color of Hollywood villainesses. Or innocent young heroines of Hollywood. Or, better still, those elusive and dangerous Hollywood femme fatales who didn't make it easy for you to know which side they were on.

This newspaper description of Elza, going so far as to paint her with bright blue eyes—though in the only surviving photo of her, taken by the police, she appears to be a dark-eyed brunette—came from the same paper that called her a "disconcerting young girl with a red soul and romantic at heart" in the spectacularly titled article "Communist of Love." This corny tone more or less ran through all the major newspapers.

If the dramatic conceit they used was simple—Good versus Evil—they went to town with descriptors. They hit you on one side with "communist fanaticism," "red terror," "degenerate sorts," "individuals with no morals"; on the other, "comely girl," "mysterious," "romantic," "innocent," "woeful." The press went so overboard with lofty and perfect formulas that, in a chronicle published in Correio da Manhã, *writer Bastos Tigre, who for reasons of professional prestige had to be strict with his style, decided to coat his own anticommunist sentiments with a metalinguistic lacquer so as not to be accused of being trite.*

Tigre explained how the press's choice of adjectives to report on crime scenes was so inflated and repetitive that the words lost meaning. He was at a loss when it came to describing the strangulation of a girl by one Cabeção. In his words: "Fierce, truculent, barbaric, wicked, cold, cruel, awful, ghastly; it was all of this, but it was mainly stupid."

You cannot argue the stupidity of the crime. Even if we take into account that it was fueled by stories with this degree of juiciness, however, the anticommunist discourse adopted by mainstream Brazilian media after the failed 1935 uprising made blatant use of hysteria. Reading the newspapers of the time, one can easily understand how Getúlio Vargas managed to turn the episode into the turning point of his career—from a weak and floundering president increasingly and blatantly defied by southern interim presidential representative Flores da Cunha, among other adversaries, to the greatest name in twentieth-century Brazilian politics. Vargas united the country against the "red enemy" very competently, and the massive support from the media occurred, as it were, spontaneously. In 1940, when Elza was dug up and her murderers brought to trial, it could have been blamed on government censorship imposed in 1937 with the Estado Novo dictatorship. But in 1936, when she was arrested, the press was still relatively "free"—despite the state of siege approved by the congress in November 1935—and the discourse was already prepared.

As Brazil scholar and future US Secretary of State John Foster Dulles wrote, "relations between the Brazilian press and the Vargas government were good." The adjective seems modest. Dulles recalls that the president welcomed a group of Rio journalists on January 9, 1936, to thank them for their support. On that occasion, the president of the Brazilian Press Association (ABI), Herbert Moses, *declared that the journalists were convinced Vargas was driven "solely by the highest principles of patriotism."*

For any journalist today, that coverage is something to be ashamed of, though there is also plenty to laugh about.

Despite this let's call it "structural unreliability," we shouldn't omit the possibility of Elza's hair actually being blond, or at least golden brown, on the day of her arrest. Anything to throw them off her scent would have been welcomed at a time when, under the command of Filinto Müller, the Federal District police had already apprehended and begun to torture the German Arthur Ewert, better known as Harry Berger, one of the plot's ringleaders, and was coming down with unprecedented ferocity on any communists, leftists, and even liberals who were easy to flush out.

Two facts suggest that the O Globo *reporter might not have been making up things. The following month, Elza herself would tell her party comrades—by then transformed into her captors and judges—that in prison in January, Romano, one of the torturers from the Central Police, pulled her hair, "saying it looked dyed." Four years later, the examination of "one hundred and seventy-five grams of exhumed hairs" from the yard in Guadalupe resulted in a report signed by medical examiner Thales Dias, of the Pathology and Microscopy Laboratory of the Rio De Janeiro Forensic Medicine Institute, which contains the following passage:*

After the hairs were washed under running water and dried completely, their brown color was verified; coloration is varied, from dark, almost black, at the proximal extremities, to light brown closer to the distal extremities.

Of course that doesn't explain those blue eyes. Contact lenses were out of the question. Those that existed since the late nineteenth century were clunky, experimental things, and though the technology underwent extraordinary advances in the 1930s, when American optometrist William Feinbloom manufactured the first plastic lenses, the technology had not developed enough to be used for cosmetic purposes.

All this about blue eyes really does seem like madness. Probably a commonplace, automatic accompaniment for the descriptor "blond," more or less the way the adjective "gross" likes to stick with the noun "error."

It took me a while to understand my obsession with setting the record straight on the color of Elza's hair on the day of her arrest. What significance was there to the truth? I ended up concluding that there wasn't any. But what bothered me about that "blond Elza" was the anything-goes suggestion it brought to the character and her story, like a metonym of the eternal uncertainty to which that young girl wound up being reduced by the tons of self-seeking discourse— anticommunist—as well as the silence, just as self-seeking—procommunist—that they poured over her.

It's amazing how little or nothing remains about Elvira Cupello Calônio the real girl, born in the interior, illiterate, deflowered at a young age by her thirtysomething boyfriend. Elza became a symbol, sign, icon, scribble, scratch, trace, and finally a gap, a blank space. They crossed her out. Where's Elza? No one saw her. Elza who? That Elza? There came a day when the two sides—both the ones frantically waving the banner of victims of monsters and the ones who murmured into the darkness "she got what she deserved"—all of a sudden grew tired of that little game. Understandable. They were more than just tired. They were fed up, disgusted. There wasn't anything more there. In its pure state, any rhetoric with no real support has an expiration date. That was when the name Elza became unpronounceable. Or at least in extremely poor taste.

The strong working-class history of Sorocaba gave significant bibliographic rewards, with books by local historians Adalberto Coutinho de Araújo Neto and Carlos Carvalho Cavalheiro. I consulted both, whose authors kindly met with me, but, just like the city's records offices, no one could tell me what I hadn't already found out about their famous—or infamous—fellow citizen. Araújo Neto explained that, in researching his book on the working class, Sorocaba operária, he wasn't bothered with names and individual stories: "I tried to emphasize the working class itself." Which is fair. In any case, Elza left there too early to leave her mark.

Emblem of oblivion, the folder with the name Elvira/Elza kept in the Public Archives of the State of Rio de Janeiro, at Botafogo Beach, where the records from the old Special Commission of Public and Social Security (DESPS) were kept, doesn't contain a single document apart from her photo—the same one as always, the only one, the unorthodox half-profile mug shot in which, under the usual harsh light, Elza looks very far from deserving the unanimous compliments she once reaped thanks to her grace and beauty. This empty—or rather, emptied—folder is intriguing. Negligence? Carelessness? Always a possibility. But the motive might not be so inadvertent.

The most glaring of Elza's absences certainly shouldn't be attributed to innocent ignorance. It pulsates like a sun in negative in the heart of the book Velhos militantes: depoimentos, by Ângela de Castro Gomes (editor), Dora Rocha Flaksman, and Eduardo Stotz. The book comprises lengthy interviews with four old leftwing militants. One of them is Eduardo Xavier, known as Abóbora, heard for a total of six hours between September and October 1986, when he turned eighty-seven. Abóbora, who as a boy immigrated to Brazil from Portugal, was one of those convicted for Elza's death—the one who, according to some versions, fainted as Elza struggled in a whirl of arms and legs, the little clothesline sunk in the flesh of her *neck by Cabeção's strong hands. There was no more noteworthy or remarkable moment in Abóbora's life. Not in his public profile or— one can suppose—in his private affairs. But, over six hours of conversation, his interviewers somehow achieved the feat of ensuring Elza did not come up for even one minute. Not even for a second. As if she'd never existed.*

Where's Elza?

No one's seen her.

After his first meeting with Xerxes, Molina returned to the scratched car and headed to his rented apartment in Botafogo Beach. His girlfriend—"*Mine, mine*," he'd repeat to himself, like a schmuck, whenever some guy nearly dislocated his neck watching her pass by—had agreed to sleep over that night, which was rather rare. Camila said the apartment depressed her. Molina lived in a dim and dusty one-bedroom. Precarious stacks of books had turned the tiny four-hundred-square-foot area into an obstacle course after spilling over from three metal bookcases that had collapsed under the excess weight. An old, bulging television, with a sofa in front, was all that kept his living room from looking like the depository of a run-down used-book store. No pictures or posters on the walls, no decorations of any kind—no lamp, family knickknack, photo, rug, throw pillow, nothing. The bedroom was marginally better: aside from the bed and computer desk, purely functional items, there was a valet stand with some hats and caps from another time that came close to humanizing the environment. But it was just a threat. Molina couldn't argue with her on this matter. The whole place really was depressing. Just like him.

While he waited for Camila, he turned on the computer and Googled "Elza Fernandes." The search engine pulled up several pages, all of them virtually identical. Variations of the same short text, written in a fanatical anticommunist tone, told the story of a naïve, illiterate teenage girl who in 1935 had been the lover of the Brazilian Communist Party's head honcho. In the hue and cry that followed the party's infamous failed coup, she was suspected of cooperating with police and was cowardly strangled by the comrades of that exotic credo. Then her little, youthful body, jackknifed by brute force, was buried under a mango tree in a suburban Rio backyard. And then, voilà—there you have it, ladies and gentlemen! Out comes the rhetoric. To think what subhuman people we almost had in charge of our country! What a catastrophe we escaped thanks to the government's decisive action and our glorious armed forces! The look of the sites mirrored the simplicity of their content: besides the text there was only a black-and-white passport-sized photo of a girl looking sad, uncouth, or distrustful, or maybe all three. Wistful eyes, short hair, not even remotely beautiful. Molina was confused. This was Elza, the muse of the extreme right? What was Xerxes driving at?

He typed, "Xerxes + communist." Then, "Xerxes + PCB." There was no trace of the man on the Internet.

Then he remembered the sealed manila envelope, which he'd thrown on the living-room couch on his way in. After pulling out a can of beer from the fridge, he sat down and opened the envelope. It was filled with books: *Olga*, by Fernando Morais; *Camaradas*, by William Waack; and *Revolucionários de 1935*, by Marly Vianna. There were also two CDs, which, judging by the ballpoint-pen writing on the cover of the first, contained a copy of case number 1381 of the National Security Tribunal of 1940, which convicted Elza Fernandes's murderers. Then, shaking the envelope to make sure it was empty, the most precious of its contents fell onto the couch: a stack of bills held together with a paper clip. Molina counted the money. It was a third of what he had agreed on with Xerxes—a whole month's advance.

When Camila rang the bell, Molina opened the door freshly showered, wearing his best clothes.

"We're going out for dinner," he announced.

They went to Luigi's, a family-style trattoria on São Salvador Square, and ordered pasta with Chilean red wine, a prudent spending spree considering his position as formerly nearly destitute. He'd decided to wait for Camila to finish her second glass of wine before telling her he had scratched her car. In the meantime, sopping piece after piece of homemade Italian bread in extra virgin olive oil and scarfing it down like a maniac, he spoke with uncharacteristic verve about Xerxes, Elza, Prestes, a story full of blood and pain that Camila, a bright history student, surely knew better than him. *Ah, but not for long,* thought Molina, happy to see the way his girlfriend's enormous eyes, her most striking feature, dilated with enjoyment and curiosity—those perfectly black cherries, as black as the short Louise Brooks bob that framed her pale face.

All of a sudden Camila cried out, "Ooh! Xerxes is old enough to have met Cobra!" Her outburst drew looks from the surrounding tables.

"Biblically even," agreed Molina, thinking, *Mine, mine.* But he was slightly taken aback. How could that not have dawned on him yet? Lately, that was all Camila talked about. It should have been clear from the beginning. He had been hired to write about the same era that one of Rio de Janeiro Federal University's top history students had been researching for her senior thesis, applying herself with a seriousness disproportionate to the institutional weight of the project. Ercília Nogueira Cobra, the São Paulo feminist whom Camila called Cobra, had become his girlfriend's obsession. "The bravest woman in the world," she would say. So brave that Molina secretly believed Cobra was a few inches short of a yard. The skinny brunette earned a bit of fame at the time for doing something akin to entering the red-and-black Flamengo stronghold in the stands at Maracanã stadium wearing a Vasco jersey: in the Brazilian Old Republic, she preached and practiced free love in the most ostentatious way possible, paying out of her own pockets and signing her real name on two shockingly honest treatises on sexuality: the autobiographical novella *Useless Virginity: Novel of an Angry Woman*, and the essay *Anti-Hygienic Virginity: Hypocritical Prejudices and Conventions*. Camila had harped on it so much that Molina had even memorized the titles.

"Do you think Elza was a feminist too?"

"I dunno, Camila. She was a little girl."

Their food arrived.

"I only know a bit about her story," said Camila, dumping grated cheese over her cannelloni. "Did she really betray the party?"

"That's what they said at the time. We'll see what the old man has to say. But there's something I'm hung up on."

Camila, with her mouth full, waited, her eyes glued on Molina as he gazed uncertainly at his spaghetti. Maybe he'd eaten too much bread. He took a sip of wine.

"On the Internet," he said, "the only people who talk about Elza are these rabid extreme right-wingers on these really horrible dinky sites."

"So?"

"So I was wondering what this old guy is up to."

"If he's a right-winger too? But isn't he a communist?"

"That's what he says."

"The plot thickens. But go easy, Mo."

Mo, yeah. That part was a little embarrassing—a guy his age being called Mo. Mo for Molina, or Mo for *amor*. It was never clear, probably both. Sometimes he had to remind himself that, out of the mouth of a girl who hadn't even turned twenty-one yet, the usage was more than natural—it was the best.

Mine, mine, mine.

"Of course I'll take it easy. Who said I was uptight?"

"Don't prejudge the man, I meant to say. I know you're a geezer from the Cold War era, but pay attention: the world today is postcommunist. History no longer fits into those little boxes, if it ever did. Get it?"

Camila flashed an adorable smile, her lips red with wine.

"Sometimes," said Molina, "I forget you were in diapers when the Berlin Wall fell."

"Right. And I sucked my big toe."

"Don't start, little lady."

"Why not?"

He could sense just how happy Camila was with his new job when he showed her the ugly scratch on the fender as they were leaving the restaurant. She didn't even care. Later on, in his depressing apartment, all was confirmed when he felt her caress his chest with her right hand, like she always did, with satiated abandonment, until she slept. In recent weeks he had speculated a decline in the intensity of the electric current in those fingers, as the rust spread through his fortysomething unemployed body and soul. He was relieved to see that the amperage had returned to normal.

The next day was devoted to reading the books from Xerxes. In his haste to form an overview of the subject, Molina adopted rather confusing methods: studying indices, browsing, reading haphazardly, sifting through as many pages as possible with the eyes of a scanner, waiting for that imaginary beam of light to stumble upon a familiar name, then reading the surrounding passage, flipping back to the index of names to follow the same character throughout the story, jumping haphazardly from one book to another to compare different versions of a particular point, going back, rereading, reading back to front, backsliding, understanding one part, misunderstanding much more. This jerky path was facilitated by the fact that Xerxes had highlighted various passages in fluorescent green, like phosphorescent buoys in the pitch black. He made sure to read them all.

When next he rang Xerxes's doorbell at the end of the dark corridor loud with barking dogs and thick with the smell of frying steak, Molina had with him, in addition to his head buzzing with names and dates, the tiny digital recorder Camila had loaned him—a little machine that turned the "tapes, lots of tapes" that the old man had requested into a comical anachronism. The prospect of meeting with Xerxes again did not make him feel comfortable. There was still a nameless anxiety, a slight tightening in his gut when he rang the bell. When no one answered, he rang again, holding it longer this time. The difference was that now he'd done a quick reconnaissance of the field on which they would face one another. The past, that infinite block of pitch, no longer belonged solely to his opponent.

After the third ring, when he had already considered with a certain relief even the possibility of giving up, Maria opened the door. Without saying a word, she held it open for him.

"Good afternoon, Maria, I have an appointment with . . ."

She nodded, closed the door behind him, and slipped into the kitchen.

Molina awkwardly stood there in the middle of the living room, trying to decide if he should sit down on the same worn leather couch he had occupied on his first visit. He decided to wait standing up. To kill time, he began examining, in the darkness of the closed blinds, the old photographs in sober pewter and wooden frames that alternated with batches of books on the shelves. Two days earlier he had only taken in the overall effect of those pictures: old age, a distant past, cold matter—similar to those little portraits that adorn tombstones. Now he tried to extract other meanings from them. There was Xerxes, a young handsome guy with black hair. It was impossible not to recognize his straight nose and V-shaped eyebrows. He was posing all spindly among men with incredible mustaches, most of them in threadbare jackets, chopped-off pants, worn shoes. A beautiful, pristine Rio de Janeiro stood in the backdrop.

Then he noticed another Xerxes in one of the photos, standing beside Xerxes, just like him. A studio trick? Twin? Doppelgänger?

Xerxes cleared his throat, announcing his presence and startling Molina. He was wearing light green cotton pajamas; his eyes seemed deeper, his movements slower, the cane more necessary. He had aged a few years in forty-eight hours.

"Do you have a twin brother, sir?"

The old man struggled to make the few steps that separated him from his plaid armchair. He slowly melted into it and stayed there for a moment, motionless, eyes closed, as if trying to subdue a sharp pain. Maybe he was just catching his breath.

Finally he opened his eyes and said, "Dead. Like everyone else. Everyone has died. Turn on the recorder."

Molina obeyed, and the man began to speak. Soon Molina realized that neither Xerxes's voice nor his mind had aged one minute. They might have been even stronger, in contrast to the dying body from which they sprang forth.

"In 1934 I was twenty years old," said Xerxes. "I worked as a proofreader at the *Jornal do Commercio* newspaper, and I was an anarchist. The anarchism was my uncle's influence—my mother's brother, João Mateus, a tailor, whom I worked with when I was a lad. I thought my uncle's talk was nice; I felt there was a dignity to him, a certain loftiness that I didn't see in other people. I thought that liberation was above all an individual stance, something almost existentialist—if we can make use of that anachronism. At least that was how I understood the conversations between João Mateus and his friends. They were pure anarchists; they didn't associate with anarcho-syndicalists. But anarchism, the cornerstone in the formation of the Brazilian working class at the turn of the century, was in decline by then. In 1934, having already given up on the trade of tailoring, something I was never very good at, I went to work at the offices of *Jornal do Commercio* and met Luiz. Luiz was from the party. He approached with the recommended caution in those situations. Commenting on news we had just proofed about the grain harvest in the Soviet Union or the like, he gradually began introducing social issues, probing me. We discovered we had some things in common: the private revolt, the certainty that there was something very wrong with the distribution of wealth in this world. But then Luiz asked me if I'd ever read anything by the great and much-missed Lenin, at that time dead for ten years. I replied that I knew roughly about his thinking, individual phrases published in the papers. Luiz was outraged, telling me, 'So you don't know anything about dialectical materialism, comrade!' He told me that an intelligent young man with good instincts such as I needed to discover scientific socialism, that the world was on the brink of a wonderful transformation—a classless society was the inevitable fate of the species. I found that conversation more exciting, more practical, more modern than the ones I'd heard around João Mateus. Not to mention that Luiz just in passing, as someone not looking for anything but clearly looking, mentioned female comrades. Yeah, women. João Mateus's group didn't have women, or rather, some of them had wives, but they were women who stayed at home taking care of the children. They weren't part of the group; they weren't comrades. They weren't even pretty like some of the ones that Luiz talked about with a lustful expression that seemed exceptionally vulgar to me. The Red Aid, one of the organizations that served as the legal front for the party's activities, was full of 'skirts,' he used to say, elbowing me in the ribs. Underneath those skirts were petticoats, and underneath the petticoats, panties, and the truth is that the burning revolutionary passion created all of the conditions—Luiz nearly drooled as he said this—all of the conditions, comrade Xerxes, for the dialectical implementation of these steps. It was somewhat comical, I'll admit, that mixture of politics and lewdness, but I was young, and I was hooked. Luiz may not have been an orthodox communist, but he knew the primer well and lent me books—all the usual ones, Lenin, Stalin, all translated from Spanish, that kind of thing. I read with great intensity. I found some things difficult, but I understood most of it. One August night, a month after our first conversation, Luiz took me to my first meeting. He told me, 'I'm not Luiz there, remember. My name is Romero.'

"The meeting was held at one of their homes, Antônio's, in Rio Comprido. Everybody used nicknames. One was Claúdio. The other, Guarani. I, they told me, would be Romeo. Romero and Romeo. I found that odd. I'd been brought by Romero, so I was Romeo? But I thought it was better to keep quiet. No lady comrades to be seen. I don't remember very well everything that was discussed, but I know it seemed petty, small, clumsy. I was expecting a high-caliber philosophical debate on the fates of humanity, and those people were talking about how to raise funds to hand out a pamphlet, who would write the text, if it should say 'Workers of the World, Unite!' or 'All Power to the Soviets!' This issue divided the group. One detail I'll never forget: Claúdio was on one side, Guarani and Antônio on the other, Luiz-Romero was undecided. I thought about suggesting the text just have both slogans and be done with it, case closed, end of discussion. Why not if both seemed fine, I thought? Even though I didn't quite know what went along with being a Soviet. Thankfully, I didn't have time to open my mouth. Suddenly, the doorbell rang and everyone jumped from their chairs, shooting glares at Antônio.

There was even one, Guarani if I'm not mistaken, a scrawny guy with black curly hair, who ran to the window like he was going to jump. I was worried—we were on the third floor. But Antônio calmed down everyone and said he was expecting a lady comrade. A most trustworthy lady comrade, he stressed, in the face of the overall bad mood. The bell rang again. 'And this little sweetheart of yours had to come right in the middle of our meeting?' scolded Luiz, my debauched friend, with a severity that even I found odd. 'She's not my sweetheart. You don't know what you're talking about; don't even joke about something like that,' stammered Antônio, pale, before leaving the room to open the front door. He returned a minute later in the company of a little brunette with short hair, a smiling face, very alive. The first lady comrade I met. 'Good evening, good evening, good evening, good evening,' she repeated in a singsong voice, greeting each of those present. 'I'm Elza.'"

Xerxes grabbed the glass of water on the tray held out by Maria, who had entered the room with her phantom footsteps. He took a half-dozen short sips, with each sip swallowing one of the pills that had been lined up in a row on the tray.

"Elza didn't stay there longer than a couple of minutes. She had come just to pick up a book, as I understood it. She left after repeating that single-file line of good evenings to us, and Antônio showed her out. When he returned, everyone looked at him and then at each other with mischievous expressions, scoundrel grins stretching to the corners of their mouths. Then Antônio, looking annoyed by it all, said, 'Elza Fernandes is comrade Miranda's companion.'"

"The sentence was like a downpour coming down on a bonfire. I was a greenhorn and didn't know who comrade

Miranda was, but judging from everyone's faces around the table when Antônio said that, there was a funny mixture of alarm, embarrassment, and haste to change the subject. I quickly understood he was a big shot. Later, Luiz confirmed my assumption. I hadn't heard, but Miranda had just been elected secretary-general of the party in the most dazzling ascent of its history. He was the bigwig, the head honcho, and they said, according to Luiz, that this was just a simple question of fairness: a brilliant guy, bold, fiery public speaker, refined in theory, and experienced in practice—the best of us all, many lengths ahead. Perhaps that piqued my curiosity about the girl with short hair and sprightly gait who walked as if she had springs in her shoes. All I know is that the memory of her followed me for a long time after that meeting in Rio Comprido. In some obscure and even ridiculous way, but by no means less powerful, that graceful little brunette seemed to confirm for me the absurd portrait of communism as a sexual heaven on earth that Luiz had painted for me in his proselytizing. I began almost unwittingly to imagine a hierarchy in which the best-quality women were reserved for the party bigwigs. So Elza Fernandes, by Marx, could only be the crème de la crème. I even dreamt about her for nights on end, sweaty, gasping, incomplete dreams.

"I'm aware that all of this must sound silly to a young man today, but you must not forget, my boy, that we were in the 1930s. Even among the working class, who cultivated a much healthier and natural relationship with these matters than the puritanical petty bourgeoisie, even in this environment the life of a healthy young buck wasn't easy. Aside from *professionals*—and I assure you, I never made use of them—the game was really tough. Not that it was impossible to score a goal here and there. Goals were scored. But the guy had to be prepared for the backlash from the referee or opposing fans. Forced marriages, suicides with Lysol, jail— all this was on the horizon. No wonder most of us preferred to do without."

Xerxes paused as if he were waiting for some response. It took a few seconds for Molina to understand that his grimace, a ghastly grin, was a mischievous smile.

"I can imagine."

The old man's eyes got lost on the bookshelf above Molina, who assumed he was looking for a book. But then he realized that Xerxes was searching for a memory in the archives of his head—a depository that was starting to seem to Molina comparable to the National Library.

"*King Kong* was playing in Cinelândia," Xerxes continued, "a late Saturday afternoon matinee. I went alone, as I often did. I was crazy about the movies. I'd already seen that picture —it was a rerun—but I had nothing better to do and thought it would be a good idea to see it again and try to decipher the wondrous optical tricks that, in those days, we still hadn't been taught to call special effects." He cracked another grin, accompanied this time by a hoarse chuckle. "Can you imagine, my boy, a time when *King Kong*—the one with Fay Wray and that grotesque puppet filmed in stop-motion, more stopping than motion—can you imagine a time when *King Kong* was a technological marvel, a wonder that mesmerized crowds in a dark theater? If you can't, if you don't have this capacity for abstract thinking, then I'm afraid you won't understand much of my story."

"Well, sure," started Molina. But it must have been a rhetorical question, as Xerxes stopped him short, not the least bit interested in his reply.

"Understanding, or rather *feeling*, the blast of novelty that little RKO picture represented for us as if you had actually been there is an intellectual exercise comparable to breathing the air we breathed back then—and now, I don't know if you noticed, but I'm talking politics again. It is hard to explain this to someone from the twenty-first century; these folks who are always ready to kill or be killed over a traffic tiff but never for their ideas. Oh no, never that. No belief—unless you're a Muslim terrorist perhaps—no belief justifies the loss of absolutely anything, let alone life. Passion for a pack of soccer hooligans, sure! In the name of that, sure, someone kills, slaughters, dies every Sunday and sometimes in the middle of the week. But ideology, political beliefs, worldview? Bah! You're funny, aren't you? It's hard to explain that world to you, my world, but I'm going to try."

Xerxes's patronizing tone stung Molina. He wanted to tell the old man to go easy on him. "I read John Reed's book," he almost shouted.

"As a consequence of the First World War, starting in the '20s, the political atmosphere had been polarizing increasingly toward extremes: the center, classical liberal democracy, all of a sudden became pathetic, laughable. And Brazil, where democracy had never been very liberal, much less classical, Brazil mirrored this in its own way, in the unpopular and repressive governments of Arthur Bernardes and Washington Luís. But it was in Europe that all hell broke loose between right and left, the center shrinking more and more, like an iceberg melting until it becomes just an ice cube to put in your whiskey."

Sitting in his armchair, long hands resting on the handle of his cane, Xerxes seemed to grow, electric and stiff, the same as when Molina had met him two days earlier.

"Everyone knows, and even you must know, that there was a moment in the twentieth century when the value of a human life hit bottom: in the '40s, with the slaughter of World War II, when sixty million people were turned to ground beef. But for the price of flesh to fall to such a degree on the international market of souls, another decade had to have come before it, in which not so many people died, but when the philosophical foundations, as we'll call them, of the slaughterhouse were being laid. I'm speaking of course of the 1920s and above all the 1930s. Ah, the '30s. The heyday of the great totalizing ideas of social engineering, both left-wing and right-wing. A time of compressing the center, flattening humanism, pulverizing belief in individual freedom as a supreme value—all this, which could be called petty bourgeoisie ideology, to use our preferred platitude of the time, all this shrank to the point of seeming ridiculous. We, the young people back then, were modern, futurists, steel willed. We demanded solutions of steel. The old, faltering bourgeoisie were of no use to us anymore. Big systems governed the future of humanity. Totalitarian, rational, just states, planners. Nations forged in war, fueled by death. Because in the end it would be a war between enemies so irreconcilable they would have to kill themselves. The class war to end all class wars. The world was too small for those two conceptions of humanity."

Molina shifted on the couch, and Xerxes must have interpreted this as unease, because he stared at him with his beady green eyes and said, "You mustn't imagine that I am in any way wishing to establish a moral sameness between black and white, Red and Green, good and evil. No! For me a fascist and a communist will never be interchangeable. *By Althusser,* my boy. Nothing could be further from my thinking. The communist is a much better person; there is no comparison. I solemnly declare here that if the Red and the Green faced one another a thousand times, I would be Red a thousand times over. This doesn't impede me from recognizing that the life of an individual was just as expendable for one system as for the other. How could it be different if the two engaged in a war that was so grand, so definitive, over nothing less than the future of the species? As Michael Corleone said, 'Who's being naïve, Kay?' In other times, like yours, people have been less willing to grant such power to the state and so little to the citizen. Not in the '30s. This is the atmosphere you should be breathing here: one in which a life is worth very little, worthless. Was it always that way? Well, let's agree that at that time it was worth even less than it had been worth on average over the last, let's say, two hundred, two hundred fifty years. Before that I don't dare speculate about how much a human life was worth on the market, but I suppose it wasn't much, even just for health and hygiene reasons. Now imagine, if you can, a communism without any cognizance of the monstrosities of Stalin, pure Leninism. Imagine it's still 1930. This communism that doesn't yet know about the crimes of the great mustachioed villain that are down the pike, a generous bet. If you were young, called upon, if you had a certain sense of solidarity and adventurous disposition like I had, it was an irresistible bet. Socially and historically. Understand this: the twentieth century brought a breath of fresh air, a dizzying promise of change. A promise that would wind up being fulfilled, incidentally, though far from the way we expected. Communism without Stalin, only Lenin, is like the militarist right without Hitler, only Napoleon. Believe me, the world was much better before these guys. It was a tough learning experience, my boy, that brutish time. One villain with a handlebar mustache; one with a tiny, square mustache; a war that would divide history into before and after. When Gorbachev came along later and the Wall fell, it was strange, very strange, like someone had pulled out the rug from under me. But this affects me as a communist. Someone who had believed his entire life that, with all the mistakes that had been made, good or bad, communism was a project of social engineering, no turning back—it was eternal, more advanced, inevitable. To see all this fall down like a house of cards was a decisive historical moment for me. For us. But the World War was different. It makes a difference still today. It divided the entire history of humanity, of each of us, no matter the creed, whether one knows it or not. Violently. As an ax splits a log, understand? Spraying splinters everywhere."

Xerxes stopped to catch his breath. Molina remained in stunned silence.

"All of that because of *King Kong*, huh? We'd better take it slowly. We're still in Cinelândia; it's October 1934, a muggy Saturday evening. It looks like it's going to rain, and I'm leaving the movie theater when I meet Elza."

Her name hung there gleaming in the air, among the thin beams of sunlight that filtered through the blinds. The afternoon was growing old, and Molina hadn't realized it. In Xerxes's living room, he felt disembodied, more like an idea. He thought about the blobs of amber in Tralfamadore, freezing moments in an eternal present. It was like they were inside one of those blobs, surrounded by others in crisscrossing corridors, going in and out of sight in a translucent and infinite museum called Time. A blob like the one in the fifth episode of *The Twilight Zone*'s first season when Martin Sloan finds his childhood and becomes a cripple forever.

He needed to ask the old man if he'd read Vonnegut.

Xerxes repeated her name more slowly, drawing out the two syllables: Elll-zzzaa. Molina thought he heard a sigh. Suddenly concerned with the permanence of all these words, he checked the recorder on top of the small coffee table, next to the big opal ashtray. The red light was still on.

"Early each evening," said Xerxes, "a salty breeze would come up from Guanabara Bay and blow through Rio Branco, ruffling the trees, just to remind us that in spite of appearances and the efforts by Pereira Passos, Brazil's own Haussmann, we were in Rio and not in Paris. But that evening the breeze was more than a breeze; it was almost a gale. I already said that it was setting up to rain. Standing alone in the door of the movie theater, blocking the way of those leaving, Elza seemed unsure about which direction to take in life after the death of that ape. She was wearing a light blue dress that flapped in the wind. She recognized me right away. Not knowing what to do after introducing myself—as Romeo, I had this presence of mind—I offered her a cigarette. I smoked a lot back then, always that brand Noel wrote about in that samba song, Liberty Ovals. Expensive cigarettes, a luxury I granted myself. I never said I was immune to petty bourgeois diversions. Elza refused my gift but still reciprocated with a smile that filled me with joy and panic. It was a smile that was too open, too pretty; I wasn't used to it. I thought I had a chance with her, and I was afraid. My legs were shaking. I jammed both my hands into my pants pockets to hide it. I asked if she wanted to get an ice cream at Cavé.

"Elza had a relatively deep voice, harmonic, but when she got excited about something, which happened frequently, her voice tuned up and she'd let out some very funny squeaks. She said she'd never had ice cream, and I was sure she was making fun of me. It was only after that I learned it was true. Elza had never had ice cream. Her first ice cream was with me.

"She moved like an animal; there was something feline in the choreography of arms and legs. She wasn't beautiful, not at all. Captain Davino calls her beautiful in his book, that crook Gruber too, but she wasn't beautiful. She was cute, but her features were just normal, nice. A brunette like so many others. But Elza wasn't so many others; she was unique. Only those who knew her could understand. On the way up to Rio Branco, I floated along, warmly aware of the lustful male gazes that followed her and which at some point inevitably ended up bouncing off me with jealousy.

"I had never been in Cavé. The pastry shop and ice cream parlor founded in 1890 was far too elegant, with its French stained-glass windows and customers with their noses in the air, soirées, and English tailored suits. All that wasn't for me or for Elza, in her little baby-blue dress and flat shoes that were starting to wear out on the toe. But I was the one who felt uncomfortable inside, sitting at a small corner table. Headstrong, trying out of the corner of my eye to intercept any glances of disapproval caused by our presence, I regretted wearing my plain gray suit instead of the more dashing black one that I kept for special occasions. But how was I to know that Saturday would be the most special one of my life? Elza was oblivious to it all. She was sheer bliss, childlike excitement. Speaking loudly, too loudly for the exaggerated standards of discretion dictated by my embarrassment, she asked if it was true that the ice cream was made from snow and, if it was, how did they get their hands on snow in Rio de Janeiro? Did they import it from Switzerland, from the United States of America? How didn't it melt on the ship on the journey over? It was the first time I had a glimpse of that girl's stunning, almost miraculous lack of awareness of social class. It made you want to sit her in your lap, cradle her. Storm her from behind, bite the nape of her neck and, at the same time, protect her. I was a little dizzy. It felt like Cavé's overly ornate chandeliers were gleaming excessively with an intrusive brightness.

"Elza ordered a goblet of vanilla, an elaborate pyramid decorated with éclairs filled with milk caramel and thin wafers arranged like butterflies. She didn't even look at the menu, just pointed to the next table over and requested the same. I mentally subtracted the price of the extravagant ice cream from the money I had in my pocket. There was barely enough left over for the tram. I claimed an upset stomach, which was only half a lie, and ordered just a glass of water. Not knowing what to say as she tried to chip away at her pyramid with ravenous mouthfuls, I figured that the girlfriend of such a high-ranking communist leader must be used to hairy theoretical debates. Dying to impress her, I started to quietly recite everything I remembered from an article I'd read recently in the workers' magazine *Classe Operária* on imperialist groups fighting in Brazil: Standard Oil and Anglo-American over oil; Chargeurs Réunis and Mala Real Inglesa over navigation; coffee exporters in Santos against the São Paulo Railway; English, Americans, and even Japanese entering the country with full force, battling in São Paulo over the control of coffee and cotton, while the English, Americans, and French fought over cocoa from

Bahia. Blah blah blah. Elza looked at me in silence, her mouth smeared with ice cream. I interpreted her silence as approval of my revolutionary spirit and, leaning toward the table, I lowered my voice even more. 'Given this situation,' I said, 'it's obvious that President Vargas is more lost than a compass without a magnet. Look at the *mil-réis ouro* banknote decree, for example; it harms the English interests, deeply harms them. At the same time, the monopoly on the currency exchange favors the English and Americans and hurts the French. The man doesn't know where to turn. He's trying to go in every direction at once—that is, every direction but toward the true interests of the Brazilian people. Don't you think?'

"Elza held the spoon halfway to her mouth, tilted her head a little to the side, and said, 'If you say so. But what's a compass?'"

The old man burst into a fit of laughter that was so outrageous, Maria peered out from behind the kitchen door.

"That's right, my boy. Elza didn't know a thing. Nothing at all. Or rather, yes, she knew how to make soap out of ashes and could press a perfect crease in your clothes with an iron full of hot coals without burning the fabric or soiling it with soot. She knew a lot of things working-class women had to learn by heart. She was the daughter of a worker at the Light & Power electric company, one of eight children, she told me. She came from a town that used to be called the Manchester of São Paulo, with a larger working class than most big cities, a place called Sorocaba. But she had no polish, no political culture, and little experience with the petty bourgeois luxuries that by then the radio and especially the cinema were beginning to stuff in everyone's heads, rich and poor. Gessy Lever, the soap of the stars, and all that crap. We were right at the beginning of the avalanche of merchandise that buries everything today, and Elza looked at it with curiosity, not quite understanding what was going on. She lacked the slightest point of reference. To start with, she was illiterate. She loved going to the movies, thought Greta Garbo was the most stunning woman on Earth, but confessed to me with the utmost candor that she didn't understand a word of what was written on the screen. The subtitles meant about as much to her as newspaper headlines or restaurant menus. Unfortunately, she wouldn't live long enough to experience dubbing. The movies were a petty bourgeois pleasure, she said, quoting Bangu, a close friend of Miranda's, a product of the imperialism of the United States of America. But Elza didn't care about that, or even that she didn't understand a thing. For months on end, she dreamt about certain scenes, certain details. Garbo looking in the mirror, Claudette Colbert's hairdo, which she believed was similar to her own. Sometimes she thought it was even better not to understand what people were saying on the screen, so she could imagine only nice things.

"Elza told me all this as we strolled aimlessly through downtown Rio that Saturday evening after leaving the ice-cream parlor. She took the lead and hooked her right arm around my left arm, a gesture of intimacy I hadn't dared force but received as a blessing. I wasn't afraid anymore. The promised rain never arrived, and at one point the leaden cloak of clouds tore open magically from top to bottom, right at the point where the nearly full moon shone in the light gray sky. Then Elza snuggled closer to me, rested her head on my arm, and asked if I could teach her to read and write. She said to me, 'Miranda, you see, was trying to do that with the greatest patience, but I'm just a hardheaded moron.' But, I learned, Miranda had left her, and she had no idea what would become of her life. We arrived at the Passeio Público park, and amid the murmur of waves breaking against the rocks I heard Elza sniffling. I stroked her thicket of unruly hair with my free hand and led her to the nearest bench. Tears streaming down her face, she smiled sheepishly, saying, 'I'm so silly; don't you pay me any mind.' Then my heart swelled and the next thing I knew I was drinking Elza's tears, a girl's tears, but no longer were they the tears of Miranda's girlfriend. The joy I felt told me the future was good, the future was so good. At that moment, in the middle of the most unforgettable kisses of my life, I promised her everything. To teach her to read, to love her, and never, never, *never* let anything bad happen to her, ever."

Molina said, "So it's a love story then!"

There was no sarcasm in his words, at least not intentionally. It was a spontaneous remark, sparked by his surprise and even a sort of enchantment. Relief as well. If the old man's interest in Elza was purely sentimental, Molina reckoned, his concerns about the political implications of the story could be safely put aside.

Xerxes seemed to snap out of a deep trance. He blinked several times and looked at Molina like an entomologist examining a common butterfly, only to confirm his initial impression of dealing with a specimen devoid of any scientific or aesthetic interest.

"A love story," he said, echoing Molina's words. "They all are, son. But if you mean to say like in an afternoon TV movie, then no. Or like *Love Story*, that cancer-and-hospital tearjerker, also no. If that sort of romantic label is your kind of thing, maybe you can experiment with it as a parallel to *Romeo and Juliet.* It helps quite a bit that my code name was Romeo, remember? All you have to do is turn Elvira Calônio into Elza Capulet." Flashing a cruel grin, the old man revealed his yellowed dentures. "Notice that the initials are the same. Let's see where this path leads. Instead of enemy families from Verona, the thing that separated us was the party. How do you like that? Hmm, I guess not. Even in my wildest delusions I never believed that Elza was Juliet or that she was in love with me. She gave me some kisses I will never forget on a night she was feeling abandoned and sad. Just that. Later I found out that on the *King Kong* Saturday night, Miranda had been in Moscow doing his famous circus act, balancing balls on his nose and riding a unicycle on the tightrope all at the same time, to the enjoyment of Manuilsky and all the other Russians. What perfect timing. On the night I covered Elza in kisses, believing I'd found my true path in life, Miranda was trying, in fluent French, to lay the foundations of madness that one year later would yield the most abject insanity. Yes, tovarich, Brazil is ripe for the revolution! That's right, tovarich, we control thousands of unions from north to south! Obviously, tovarich, the army. How could we forget the army? It is, according to the latest calculations, seventy percent under our command. Perhaps seventy-one. The *cangaceiro* outlaws? Oh no, of course we won't put the *cangaceiros* aside in our unceasing work; we have representatives working at this very moment to give true Marxist-Leninist meaning to the armed front line of the peasants, *mon cher* tovarich. Blah blah blah. That's where you might need to change the Shakespearian play, my boy. I hope this doesn't confuse you too much, but Iago is a character from another story. They say Miranda turned into him during his spell in the capital of the free world, when he so debonairly made the little eyes of the Communist International grow for this enormous and incredibly interesting country, albeit semifeudal, which up until that point they had unapologetically ignored. Even so, at the end of the day maybe me being Romeo isn't so absurd. As long as I'm a Romeo who's worse than that Romeo, a one-sided Romeo. It was never clear to me what the misunderstanding was that led Elza to consider herself abandoned by Miranda, throwing herself in the arms of another as if she were holding on to a buoy in a storm. It was probably just something silly, because everything indicates that Miranda didn't see things the same way. He never believed in separation. She believed it on her own, but all he had to do was return from his trip with some shoddy gift—a piece of Soviet fabric, imagine—and that was that. Elza was crazy about Miranda. Always had been. Much to my chagrin, until her death she would never cease being crazy about him."

Xerxes fell into a sad silence. It was completely dark. Molina excused himself to go to the bathroom and, when he returned, the old man was standing waiting for him by the front door, one hand on his cane and the other on the doorknob. "See you the day after tomorrow," he said. "Don't forget to bring the recorder."

3

—

WITNESS

SEVERINO MONTEIRO DA SILVA, born in Paraíba do Norte, forty-eight years old, married, able to read and write, federal public servant, working as an investigator of the Federal District Civil Police—number 92, and serving in the Department of Explosives, Firearms, and Ammunition Inspection, resident at Rua Ada, number 56, in Piedade. In answer to the customary questions asked to establish eligibility to serve as a witness, he made no disqualifying statements. Duly sworn in as required by law and questioned about the facts regarding this investigation, he replied that some time last month, the exact date of which he was unable to verify, he received orders to report for police duty under this special precinct from his colleague Castro; that this duty would be to attend and direct some excavations at a site in order to recover human remains that had been buried; that he accompanied the aforementioned investigator Castro to a place far from Deodoro, which he later discovered was 48A Rua Maria Bastos, on Camboatá Road; that two other investigators, named Segadas and Ribeiro, went along with the deponent, and Castro and the four men, all under the same orders, directed some manual laborers, unknown to the police, in carrying out the excavation work; that the deponent knew the purpose of this work was to discover the location where Elvira Cupello Calônio, murdered in 1936 by representatives of the Communist Party, had been buried; that after the second day of work and after uncovering some holes, the group found one of them to be suspicious, which was connected horizontally to another hole, which gave off an unusual smell and where, encased in the upturned earth, one could see what appeared to be human hairs; that on orders from Investigator Castro, the work was interrupted at that point, and news of the discovery brought to this precinct by the same investigator; that on the day following the discovery, the special precinct captain appeared at the site, accompanied by several aides, including the police chief presiding over these proceedings, and the individual accused of this crime, EDUARDO RIBEIRO XAVIER, and the brother of ELVIRA CUPELLO CALÔNIO, Luiz Cupello Calônio; that the police chief overseeing this document ordered the continuation of the excavation of this hole, and this work was carried out by the deponent and the aforementioned Castro; that as such, the horizontal hole was completely cleared—dug as if it were a pit, and a human skeleton removed from there; that, as the deponent was very near, he heard Elvira's brother say that he recognized his sister by the skull that had been passed to him.

It's an astonishing scene, documented in a front-page photo in the April 17, 1940 issue of A Noite *newspaper: police chief Hugo Auler, in a white suit and panama hat, hands Elza's skull to Luiz Cupello Calônio, also a communist militant, and the poor soul's brother struggles over Hamlet-esque doubts. He immediately recognizes the skull, then immediately, before the battalion of police officers and journalists present, renounces the party.*

There wasn't the slightest doubt that the body they dug up was Elza's. If there were any doubt, however, it would have been eliminated by experts. Like the dentist Maurício da Gama e Silva, who quickly reported to the police that in the final days of 1935, at his first-floor office at 145 Avenida Rio Branco, he had treated what he believed to be a sixteen-year-old girl, who identified herself as Elza, from Minas Gerais. Her face swollen, she had an abscess in the upper-right premolar that the dentist extracted immediately. At subsequent appointments, as detailed in his testimony, he performed other work in the girl's mouth—porcelain fillings—until in early 1936, Elza stopped coming. When he read the news of the exhumation in the paper, Maurício da Gama e Silva connected the dots and volunteered to "lend his assistance in elucidating the facts." Unfortunately, he explained, a fire in his office building destroyed his records, but he was able to reconstruct her chart since, he said, he kept a perfect memory of it, "because it was a good set of teeth"— even if incomplete because her wisdom teeth or third molars had not come in yet "due to her young age."

If her dental arches weren't enough to confirm the identity of the body beyond a shadow of a doubt, there were the victim's clothes, shoes, and other accessories, which no one would need to be a relative or have a diploma in forensics to recognize. All that would have been required was some degree of interaction with her: the wardrobe of a girl in her condition wouldn't be that big, after all. The following items were collected from the hole in that yard next to the Camboatá Road and catalogued by the authorities:

A) Pair of woman's shoes, flats with black uppers, imitation snakeskin, looks like patent leather, with a brown leather (strap?) on the top, with laces measuring twenty-seven centimeters, significantly altered and hardened by time; B) Shawl reduced to various tattered pieces, indiscernible color; C) Thin cloth slip, appears to be silk, color varies from yellowish to dirty yellow, very tattered with several tears, rips easily, measuring eighty centimeters long; D) Dress, reduced to shreds, appears to be voile, brown with light purple areas, significantly altered and torn; E) Rope, five millimeters in diameter, reduced to two fragments, one twenty-three centimeters and the other twenty-seven centimeters, with a knot on the end of one of them; F) Thick cotton cloth fragment, altered, and a piece of some kind of yellow ribbon.

No, the meaning of the incongruous scene, composed by Hugo Auler and Luiz Cupello Calônio by the edge of a recently opened grave in front of a small audience, cannot be understood through the filter of police logic. What applied there was the logic of the theater. Authorities and the press attempted to take full advantage of the situation. Luiz was there to cry. So was the Portuguese suspect, Eduardo Ribeiro Xavier, whom history remembers as the most "sensitive" of Elza's murderers for having, according to his own statement and those of others, fainted at the moment she was strangulated by Francisco Natividade Lyra, or Cabeção. He must have been cast to perform a similar role—though he didn't cry, as far as we know. And we would know.

The brother of Elvira Cupello Calônio excused himself from the recently discovered gravesite to write a note addressed to Miranda, which was later forwarded to all of the newspapers:

Dearest Bonfim,

I have just witnessed the exhumation of my sister Elvira's body. I even identified her teeth and her hair. I also learned of the confession that representatives of the PCB made to the police: they murdered my sister, Elvira. In light of this I renounce my revolutionary past and put an end to my communist activities.

Your friend always, Luiz Cupello Calônio

If the script included Luiz's public renouncement from the start, or if this welcome bonus was improvised, we will never know. It is not unlikely, however, that all this had been rehearsed beforehand. Elza's brother's situation with the police was shaky. Less than one month later he would be accused of having participated, under orders from party leaders, in another episode of vigilante justice a few years earlier, this one thwarted—the gunning down of Bernadino Pinto, or Dino Padeiro, also suspected of treason, who was shot at close range but against all odds survived.

When Molina later thought back about those days working with Xerxes, his prevailing feeling would be one of plenitude. This was so wrong it was even humorous. Soon he would discover that his understanding of what was going on around him was anything but full. He was trying to gaze at a giant mural with his nose stuck in one corner. The bottom left, let's say. His field of vision was filled with the roughness of the brushstroke the painter had used to represent a horse's right-rear hoof. From just that, how can you guess the bluish meadows and the patches of woods, the low clouds and the rolls of black smoke, the bell tower in the distance, the curve of the river, and the two thousand soldiers in epic battle?

For a guy who for years had done everything in his power to be more of an observer—an ultracritical if not to say surly observer—and less of an actor in this human comedy, this was not a flattering realization. But the worst was knowing Camila's mother had been the first one to take a few steps back and appreciate the scope of the mural, when he was still snared where he had stuck his nose.

Given Camila's distaste for his place, Molina did not usually turn down his girlfriend's invitations to sleep over in her room, in the spacious apartment on Rua do Russel, overlooking Aterro do Flamengo park, that she shared with her mother and teenage sister. There was only one unpleasant aspect to this arrangement: Laura, Camila's mother. In her fifties, she acted the part of an old hippie, with long, reddish hennaed hair and the air of someone who'd smoked more than one joint too many. When she was in a good mood, she treated him with ironic condescension, and with open hostility when she was in a bad mood. She obviously disapproved of her daughter's choice. Camila could have any man she wanted, but she opted for a plain guy twice her age. Luz—short for Luzia—the baby sister, might have also agreed with her mother's opinion, though it was hard to be sure what a nearly autistic teenager eternally plugged in to her iPod was thinking.

There was also the good side. In that beautiful neoclassical building with a pink facade in the geographical and spiritual vicinity of the Hotel Glória, Molina could make love to Camila on a sprawling bed in sheets that smelled of fabric softener, surrounded by a profusion of those signs of life that were missing in his own apartment: photos of Camila at all ages on a corkboard; a doll collection on a sideboard from an antique shop; an acrylic lamp shaped like a palm tree that Molina deemed the most kitsch thing he'd ever seen; a Takamine acoustic guitar and Fender bass accompanying an old Giannini amp; a Balinese batik in shades of green and violet stretched across the wall over the bed; a small rectangular aquarium with white pebbles where a blue betta named Zeb lived; a computer with an LCD monitor adorned with Mickey Mouse ears. All this and a whole bunch of odds and ends, little music boxes, perfume bottles, a collection of pens, handmade crafts, and an encyclopedic variety of throw pillows—round, rectangular, shaped like stars, hearts, amoebas, beans, sausages. Ah, and books too. Lots of them. The difference was that they remained on the shelves, tamed and organized by subject. In their relationship, Camila made it clear who was in charge.

He arrived with two bottles of a good, midpriced Chilean wine. His message with the gift was also twofold: he proclaimed he had a job again and therefore expected to be treated with the respect due to men who earned money, and he communicated to Laura that her weakness was no secret, but that it was fine—he wasn't there to judge her. Why not just toast together? Camila's mother didn't go one night without drinking, and when there was no wine or beer she attacked some bottles of whiskey she kept tucked away in her room.

They chatted in the kitchen—Luz on one side of the table, a dyed streak of green in her hair, listening to music and doing her homework; Camila on the other, slicing tomatoes for a salad; Molina stood next to the door. Laura opened the first bottle and poured three glasses.

"Hey, I want some too," said Luz.

The teen's mother raised her eyebrows but grabbed a fourth glass from the cabinet, which she filled with a third of the generosity dispensed to the others.

"To the job," Laura toasted.

For the first time, Molina felt comfortable in their home. He didn't hold a grudge against Laura. In spite of everything, she accepted better than most the presence of the guy who was screwing her daughter—better than he would, if he were in her shoes.

Laura started to tell Camila a long story her hairdresser had told her that afternoon. She always managed to exclude Molina completely from the conversation without seeming rude, using only a look and the tone of her voice. It was a talent he respected. But the gossip that overflowed in the hair salon over knitting became, in a few minutes, a stretched-out and boring story, though by involving a run-over poodle, a bogus beggar, a woman suspected of incest, and a wedding dress that was never finished, it came close to being interesting. Molina had the impression that Laura, in the middle of her story, realized it wasn't working as well in her kitchen as it had in an atmosphere impregnated with nail-polish remover, and she finally trailed off.

Luz didn't participate in any of it, lost in a world of her iPod and geometry problems. Every once in a while she would let out shrill cries, accompanying the music only she could hear—*"Oh yeah, baaaaby! Gimme gimme!"*—which everyone did their best to ignore.

Laura stuck a frozen store-bought lasagna in the microwave. She always had a supply in the freezer. When it became clear that she wasn't going to finish her story, Camila—*mine, all mine*—moved to include Molina in the conversation. Cutting a cucumber into transparently thin slices, she told her mother that he was working on a major book. Laura questioned this with just her eyes and a crooked grin. A *major* book, Camila insisted, and started to talk about Xerxes, totem, sphinx.

"You're interviewing this old man?" Laura said as she finally turned to him.

"More or less," said Molina. "He gets to talking, I don't even need to ask anything. I'm recording it all."

"He doesn't know how to write?"

"I imagine he writes very well. He's incredibly articulate, an intellectual. But I think that in this process of remembering he would rather have someone speaking for him, a qualified listener."

"Since when are you an expert on left-wing history?"

"I'm not, Laura." Molina was surprised by her tone. Should he have bought four bottles? "What are you driving at, *Mom?*"

Mom: good one. She hated that.

"Nothing, Molina. It just seems to me that this job of yours is being someone's secretary and not a writer. Nothing wrong with that, of course. Transcribing interviews is a worthy job like any other."

"Mother," protested Camila, "give him a break!"

"What's wrong with what I said? It would only be wrong if Molina, from inexperience in these boorish political matters, stumbled into a story he doesn't understand properly and played the helpful fool. But apart from that, it all sounds great!"

"Don't worry, Laura dear. I read *Das Kapital* and *Mein Kampf* in German. I liked the first one better. You?"

Chopping onions, Camila started to laugh.

Molina tried not to show it, but Laura's comment hurt him. He wasn't, and never had been, a political creature. Like a lot of people his age, he'd gone through a phase of enchantment with the student movement, which at that time, back in the mid-'80s, fed off the energy of being reestablished after the military dictatorship. A belated, repressed echo of the legendary unrest that was brutally suppressed in 1968, that energy proved insufficient to galvanize the students for very long. Molina's revolutionary appetite also didn't last. At the end of the decade, the air that he and his friends were breathing was different, laden with cynicism and disillusionment with collective action and traditional politics. They were looking for jobs, and inflation was breathing down their necks; the city grew seedier day by day as an idiot declared the end of history as they knew it, and AIDS sent the world into mourning. The worst was President Sarney sharing the spotlight with Thatcher and Reagan on the nightly news. All of them in a single sentence—it was hard to imagine a shadier gang of characters.

A few years before the Wall fell, when the countdown on the monstrosity's cement and barbed wire had already begun, though no one knew it yet, cynicism hadn't completely won the game. In those days of transition, being some sort of militant—"Think about Brazil," they used to say—was still as natural for students as, say, screwing around, smoking weed, drinking cheap wine, or packing in the Candelária church to demand direct elections from a regime that was dying, or worse yet, already dead, rotting in the public square. But even amid the fever of such an exciting historical moment, Molina already felt like an embarrassment around his classmates who declared themselves as deeply political, professionals divided up by sects or *tendencies*, blindly obeying a shadowy set of attractions, repulsions, alliances, accusations—a secret web of love and hate that seemed to only make sense to them, if it made sense at all. For others, mere sympathizers relegated to the outer edges of the centers of decision making, it needed to be seen as a mystery: the more abstract it was, the more important, and the more incomprehensible, the more daunting. Making the leap to broad disillusionment with politics wasn't difficult, not even *deliberate*. It seemed natural, part of the process of growing up. Molina was never so naïve that he didn't know, even without thinking carefully about the subject, that such a decision was only personal in a limited sense. Restricted to a narrow color palette, Molina's decision was more dependent on murky underground historical currents than pop culture's belief in the ultimate freedom of the individual would care to admit. The irony of the situation did not escape him altogether: the era of exaggerated individualism in which the twentieth century culminated had very little, really almost nothing, to do with individual decisions. It was mass individualism.

The microwave beeped four times, heralding the end of its work. At that moment, on the small television in the kitchen Molina saw the country's bearded president, a former union leader, praising General Médici's government that tortured and killed so many people. Had he heard him correctly? Luiz Inácio Lula da Silva's diction was poor, but unfortunately he'd understood him. He felt the wine churn in his empty stomach. A cycle was coming to a close—or was it a trick? At that moment history seemed to him a long drawn-out joke. Very, very drawn-out, like human limbs pulled slowly on medieval torture devices. It wasn't a funny joke at all, though he distinctly heard a hearty laugh tear through the night in Glória.

4

—

Antônio Maciel Bonfim, from the state of Bahia—also called Américo or Adalberto Fernandes, but more commonly known as Miranda by his Brazilian comrades, and Queiroz or Keiros among the Soviets—occupies a special place in the history of the Brazilian left: he is the ultimate traitor, the highest-ranking agent provocateur, the magnificent backstabber, son of a bitch number one.

After deceiving the Comintern strategists with his wildly optimistic reports on the progress of Brazilian political and social movements, the secretary-general of the PCB still found a way one year later, after the failure of the uprising he maliciously instigated, to send the entire leadership of the plot to prison, ratting them out one by one—Brazilians and foreigners—and bringing on the death of his underage girlfriend, an ignorant girl who naïvely became a pawn in his duplicitous game. Elza was the first to pay for his sins.

The story of Miranda, the one casting him as a megavillain, carries that contagious power of persuasion that forgoes evidence. It is a characteristic common to so many accusations of treason throughout political history: suspicion arises, and suspicion is all you need. Anyone who dares to point out their suspicion as merely suspicion immediately becomes suspect. Stalin lived his entire life off this ploy.

Born to a family of farmers in the Bahia countryside in 1905, Antônio Maciel Bonfim managed to become a teacher, and first joined the fleeting—and ideologically confused—League of Revolutionary Action, founded by Luís Carlos Prestes in 1930. Two years later he was in the PCB, beginning his rapid rise that would eventually take him to the party's highest-ranking position in mid-1934.

There are two basic explanations for this expeditious climb. For those who give greater weight to context, the PCB—a "division of the Communist International," at the time something all its officers were all too proud to point out—had in recent years been subjected to waves of forced renewal in order to adjust to new Stalinist demands. By 1930 the group that had been at the helm since the party's founding in 1922 had fallen from grace with Moscow, accused of intellectualism, petty bourgeois diversions, and other such deadly sins. "The campaign for 'proletarianization' took on such connotations that, in meetings of certain bodies, intellectuals were denied voting rights," noted the old militant Moisés Vinhas in his book on the history of the PCB, O Partidão. But the so-called workers' experiment, forcibly promoting manual laborers to positions of command, was also not very successful—secretary-generals succeeded one another in the early '30s without a single one sticking around. Suddenly, there was a void. They were looking for a course, perhaps a style. Antônio Maciel Bonfim knew exactly how to take advantage of the moment. At the beginning of 1934, he was national secretary of the organization. By July he was elected secretary-general at the First National Conference of the Brazilian Communist Party.

Those who would rather highlight the role of individuals in shaping the course of history emphasize a different aspect: Miranda's dazzling, albeit controversial, personality. Naturally, a combination of the two explanations seems advisable.

"He was a really highfalutin man, much too tacky *... I have to confess he never gave me a good impression," said journalist Raul Ryff, press secretary for João Goulart, in a statement recorded in 1982 and filed at the Getúlio Vargas Foundation; Ryff had run into Miranda in prison in 1936. The same comical adjective is used by historian Anita Leocádia Prestes, daughter of Luís Carlos Prestes and Olga Benário, with a few additions: "highfalutin, smooth talking, cocky, and adventurous." In his book* Camaradas, *William Waack states about Miranda that "without exception, the people who knew him described him as possessing inexhaustible self-esteem and vanity, but at the same time a friendly person, with the gift of gab."*

There is no debate: Miranda had a real mouth on him. The lips that wooed young Elza into bed (as O Globo *put it the day after his arrest, "in his spare time he also plays the dangerous sport of Don Juanism") were the same lips that seduced many others, albeit with less erotic objectives. But was it just that? Leôncio Basbaum, in his book* História sincera da República, *implies not. He refers to Miranda's "suspicious breakout"—supposedly facilitated—from prison on Ilha Grande in 1932 to suggest that from the very beginning he was an "agent of the police" who'd infiltrated communist ranks. Speaking of the famous claim made by General Góis Monteiro, minister of war under Vargas, that he had known of Prestes's arrival in Brazil since 1934, Basbaum says, "This knowledge must have been given to him by the secretary-general of the PCB himself, Miranda."*

Must have been given . . . *The levity of the phrase becomes even more shocking when you consider there was no shortage of professional informants to perform this role—the German man they called Gruber, for example, an international double agent. However, the wounded Basbaum, one of the historic communists* removed from party leadership after Miranda and his crew took it by storm, was far from the most impartial of analysts.

The version of Miranda's story that would become predominant in the left-wing media is different: it portrays Miranda as an opportunistic windbag, shaky ideologically, who couldn't take the pressure after the uprising and melted, switching sides in the war. Prestes helped to crystallize this story, describing Miranda as a nationalist, not a Marxist. "He was a man laden with subjectivist, petty bourgeois exaggeration and felt entitled to convert his desires into reality. But when he spoke of revolution, he did not know how to prepare the working class," Prestes said in a magazine interview in 1985. This is not to say Miranda was ignorant. Quite the opposite: he was a teacher and spoke French. He was intelligent. But, "he capitulated with his arrest. He went into the army's secret service."

And now, a philosophical aside. Regardless of how ironic the "subjectivist exaggeration" criticism is coming from Prestes, it is worth noting that the Marxist nature he refuted in Miranda was also frequently denied him, the greatest name in the history of Brazilian communism. For example, in his 1962 memoir, Agildo Barata, Prestes's comrade in the insurrection and the captain who led the Praia Vermelha uprising in November 1935, referred to him, with whom he had already broken ties by that point, as follows: "Prestes never was and still is not a Marxist revolutionary; Prestes is a stoic positivist. Or if you prefer: a stoic positivist with many fatalist biases." What does this prove? Nothing beyond the ease with which the fleeting distinction of Marxist was granted or denied on the whims of convenience.

Everything suggests that Miranda wasn't exactly a master of dialectic thought. Two of Brazil's most important twentieth-century writers helped to shed some light on his elusive personality. We find the future secretary-general making a cameo in a ludicrous 1932 episode in which the PCB tried to order a young militant, Rachel *de Queiroz, who had just won over the country with her novel* O Quinze, *to change a few things in the manuscript of her second book,* João Miguel. *Namely, they wanted her to adapt it to certain revolutionary aesthetics. Newly affiliated with the party, Miranda was part of the three-person panel tasked with putting pressure on the young writer one night in a dark abandoned warehouse on the quayside in Rio. Here is how de Queiroz recalls in her memoir,* Tantos anos, *the sort of literary criticism provided by Brazilian Stalinism:*

> For example: one of the heroines, a rich, blond girl, a colonel's daughter, was a pristine damsel. The other, from a lower class, was a prostitute. I was supposed to, then, make the blond the prostitute and the other an honest girl. João Miguel, a "peasant" drunkard, killed another peasant. The one killed was supposed to be João Miguel, and the murderer would go from being a "peasant" to the master.

Horrified, de Queiroz clutched her originals and ran out of the warehouse—and the PCB—never to return. Compared to this comic snapshot, the portrait of Miranda drawn by Graciliano Ramos in Chapter 14 of Memórias do cárcere *is much richer in detail and more damning. The chapter is devoted entirely to Miranda. Based on their time together in prison, the account attempts to tear apart Miranda methodically, first introducing him shrouded in shadows in the infirmary out of sight from the other prisoners, whispering about how he is feeling terrible, worn out from the torture he underwent at the Central Police Station. But then Ramos begins to see Miranda very differently after an encounter with him in the yard. The strong young man was laughing and talkative, wearing no shirt. Hints of torture were visible—slight bruising—but Miranda*

spoke of the cuts on his feet and other wounds like they were something to be proud of. He was bragging. Ramos remembers how
another prisoner had had all of his fingernails pulled out. It was
a violent environment, and no one turned a blind eye to that fact,
but to speak of it the way Miranda did, reveling in his descriptions,
was nothing but crass, which was made even worse by the fact that
Miranda's body did not show real signs of serious abuse.

This chapter ends with a little story that gives ballast to the
heavy suspicions that already hung over Miranda at that point.
Ramos says that one night, when the arrival of a certain young
female militant was announced, the "peculiar leader" revealed the
woman's alias for all to hear. The other prisoners couldn't believe
it. Miranda had said it loud enough so the guards could hear her
name, even the janitors. It became clear to Ramos that Miranda
knew exactly what he was doing and that he could not be trusted.

The judgment old Ramos never entirely spells out, because he
doesn't need to, is obvious. Miranda really was an oddball; there's
no denying it. Still, it's impossible to shake the feeling that, were it
not for the need to create a scapegoat for the humiliating defeat of a
tiny uprising, the comrades might have taken it a bit easier on him,
weighing the evidence with greater earnestness before so categori-
cally declaring him a traitor; before, as William Waack says, "mas-
sacring him," killing the girl he loved, and moving against the shell
of a man left behind with an intensive smear campaign. There are
strong signs that in those early days in jail, before Filinto Müller's
torturers at the Central Police Station, if Miranda "sang," he did
so with a much smaller repertoire than that of Rodolfo Ghioldi,
who besides leading the Argentinean Communist Party also took
the leading role in Comintern in South America—his role when
he came to Rio with his wife to participate in the uprising. "Prestes
told me it was Ghioldi who gave him up," Marly Vianna told me.

"He even wrote to Moscow reporting everything." Ghioldi died in Argentina in 1985 as a left-wing hero.

When Molina arrived, Xerxes was standing, leaning on his cane, looking for a book on the shelf. He took down from the giant wall of spines a slim volume with a blue cover. Glancing over, Molina noticed it was part of the complete works of Freud in Spanish. Xerxes leafed through it quickly before handing him the book, opened to the first page of an article entitled "*Construcciones en el análisis.*"

Molina sat down on the couch and read words at random—*arqueología, escenarios, reprimido*—while the old man, with slow, unsteady steps, paced from one corner of the living room to the other.

"Have you read Freud, my boy? Vaguely? I read him a lot, an awful lot, at one time. We took the old man seriously, second only to Marx. For me, after the Wall fell, the greatest proof that the world had really changed, that we are living in another mental geological age, is this increasingly saucy, conceited trend, mainly in English-speaking countries, to spit in Sigmund's face. You know this fad of kicking around Freud like a mangy dog, a crook? Fortunately, the world changing doesn't mean we need to change too. One day you'll figure this out on your own, if you live long enough. Getting old has its privileges. You don't mind if I walk while I talk, do you? I imagine it must be kind of annoying, but the doctors recommend it. To stimulate the circulation."

"Of course not. This your home, sir."

Xerxes stopped pacing and stared at Molina for a moment with an unreadable expression, before continuing to walk. "That is true. But as I was saying. Freud. This article you're holding has always stuck with me. It compares the work of the psychoanalyst to that of an archaeologist who has to rebuild, say, an entire Grecian urn from two or three scattered shards. How does he do it? By filling in the gaps with his imagination. He is taking a risk with this work, of course, and sometimes he really is taking a guess, a wild guess. How does he know if he has gotten it right? He doesn't know. That's just it. The litmus test is in the final result, the reconstructed urn, if it makes sense in an architectural, functional, historical, cultural sense. The closest an archaeologist can get to the truth is probability. An analyst as well. With the shards we can remember, since the full view of the urn is obscured from us."

"What do you mean by that, sir?" Molina interrupted bravely. "That the analyst here is me?"

Xerxes stopped one step away from him, his cane fixed with geometric precision on a point equidistant from his feet planted on the rug. From that angle, he looked imposing. Molina had to tilt his head up to look him in the eyes.

"You, the analyst?" Xerxes gave a short chuckle. "I hadn't thought of that, but who knows?" He laughed again, longer this time, as he returned to his green-and-purple plaid wingback armchair. It was old, but Molina had noticed during his first visit that it seemed to pop again, as if it had been reupholstered recently.

"What I was trying to say is . . . I don't really know what I was trying to say. I was trying to talk about the shards, I think. The fragments we lose forever. Here I am talking and talking, remembering and remembering, but also inventing and inventing—you should know that. There's no other way. My memory is marvelous, you should know, but there's no other way. The truth? That, I don't know. I can't swear to it. I remember, for example, that one day a car stopped in front of the boarding house where I lived, on Mem de Sá Street, and I was called down. But I can't guarantee that it was on Christmas. Why would it be right on Christmas Day? What is Christmas doing there? I don't know. But I know—in fact I'm sure of it—there were two people in that car. The driver, a tall black man wearing a panama hat, an A-shirt, and suspenders, and in the backseat a good-looking guy in a white suit who introduced himself as Miranda. My nemesis.

"I sat in the passenger seat like an automaton, my legs weak. I hated that man without ever having seen him. It was all I had left, after losing my sweetheart to him. My attempts to contact Elza in the weeks after our date in the park had proven futile. Finally, after a short, nervous conversation when I bumped into her in the street one afternoon, I was convinced that, with Miranda back up on the pedestal, my chances were nonexistent. That does not mean I was fine with it. It seemed deeply unfair that Elza, still so young, already belonged to someone and so definitively, with a deed of ownership and everything. Worse yet, her owner was someone so powerful, to whom I myself owed unrestricted allegiance as a humble party member. I don't know if this proves the flimsiness of my ideological convictions at that time, but I even thought about leaving the cause of the revolution so I could cultivate my hatred for Miranda in peace without that niggling feeling of betraying a worthy leader that poisoned my soul. Belittled me. Could Luiz really be the guilty party in that mess for enlisting me with his promiscuous talk of politics and sex? Could my militancy be rooted in this vice? I didn't think of that in those days. Elza was Elza. Inevitable, necessary. Only some years later, when it was all over, did I realize that Luiz's fetishes, his emphasis on lustful, hot companions, petticoats, and panties some-how foreshadowed the hell I had gotten myself into. In the end I didn't run away from anything. On the contrary, I wound up devoting myself even more to my tasks and mov-ing up the hierarchy. It wasn't for pure Marxist-Leninist pas-sion, you can be sure of that, though I believed in the cause and worked as hard as I could to be a good communist. Deep down, it was because I knew that if I left the party I would be even farther away from Elza. If I stuck around, who knows what could happen?

"But I wasn't expecting that to happen: Miranda com-ing to gloat. He was a determined man in his thirties, straight hair combed back, lively eyes, firm handshake. He wore an expensive-looking tie, well-shined shoes. The contrast between his refined attire and that of his driver, who, apart from the panama hat, was wearing what looked to me like a longshoreman's uniform, was almost comical. I should explain. You probably don't know this, and there's no reason you should, but at that time the party was at its height of the glorification of the working class, manual laborers. Anything that smacked of petty bourgeoisie was viewed with disdain. Speaking with grammatical correct-ness, observing subject-verb agreement, having good table manners, reading anything other than the *Classe Operária* workers' rag, any of this immediately made a guy a suspi-cious character. The former leaders of the party, intellectu-als like Astrojildo Pereira and Leôncio Basbaum, had fallen from grace. The working-class winds blew in from Moscow with the strength of a typhoon. It was on this momentum that Miranda orchestrated his crazy rise to power. Not that he was your typical proletarian. He wasn't even a worker. He'd received a well-above-average education at a school run by priests, was a sergeant in the army, worked as a teacher. But he was born to a poor family from the fields, spoke somewhat incorrectly, I suspect on purpose, and was a man identified with action. He was definitely not an intellectual. The crassest folks worshipped him. It was believed that the profound authenticity of a true revolutionary came from his roots, the humbler the better. Authenticity that dismissed and even rejected the study of theory, or was at least wary of it. We had come a long way since the days of Lenin's conscious communism. Now there was a first-rate intellectual. By that point on the Stalinist hierarchy, if the guy was a craftsman—say a tailor, as I had been when I worked with my uncle João Mateus—or, even worse, a worker who mainly used his brain, like I was by this time, at my job as a proofreader at *Jornal do Commercio*, if he didn't get his hands dirty, basically if he didn't carry around fifty-pound bags on his back or risk losing a finger in a vise, then he was a lesser person on that scale of values. A simple and even slightly naïve inversion of real life, if you stop to think about it. The workers were the aristocracy of the revolution. Most of them behaved exactly this way, reserving a disdain for the rest of humanity similar to that which an English nobleman would have for a leper peasant. That guy who was driving Miranda's car was like that. The sidelong glances that he threw back at me now and then were of utter contempt.

"I remember we aimlessly drove through the city while Miranda talked and talked. The ride seemed to have no final destination. Neither did Miranda's speech. He called me 'comrade'; occasionally, he would spring up from the backseat to punctuate some more emphatic argument with a pat on my shoulder. I was forced to periodically twist around in my seat and turn my neck to the left in order to look at him—I didn't want to seem impolite. Apart from that, I don't remember much. It would be reckless to try to retrieve the exact words said by the secretary-general of the PCB. They're blurred forever. Even his pet phrase that I hear, in my memory, punctuating his speech at irritatingly short intervals—"This is very important, comrade, very important"—even these words I don't know if I heard them from his mouth or just read them in *Memórias do cárcere* in that chapter where Graciliano makes a fool out of Miranda. Shards, didn't I tell you? The overall feeling of the conversation in the car, yes—that I am capable of reliably reconstructing: Miranda drew dream scenarios with feverish optimism, and they all involved me. He asked if I felt up to the challenge. The tone was brutally, dizzyingly patronizing. He seemed determined to turn me into an ally, all while also challenging me. That man's friendliness was an anesthetic. I didn't realize that the driver had been heading toward the Vista Chinesa overlook until we were already there.

"The man in the longshoreman's uniform stayed behind the wheel. The two of us got out and walked toward the edge of the cliff completely casually, as if it were in the script and we simply had to do it. I couldn't think straight. I remember there was a giant flock of parakeets nearby, invisible inside a huge tree, and all of a sudden something scared them—maybe our footsteps into the forest, some trampled twig, or a lizard running off, I don't know. All I know is a million parakeets exploded up into the sky with a hell of a racket, and I realized we were halfway down the slope. The sunlight bounced off the city below as if it were made of chalk. Miranda smiled; a gold tooth sparkled somewhere in the back of his mouth. He grabbed me tenderly by my jacket collar and, with a smile frozen on his lips, said that Elza had told him everything. That he'd thought of two dozen—I remember that was exactly the amount—two dozen horrible evil acts to do to her and me. That in the end he had decided to forgive Elza, because these things happen, because we were both young. But as for me. Ah, as for me: if I laid another finger on his lover again, my next trip to the Vista Chinesa overlook would be much less pleasant. Miranda pointed to the chasm below and said, 'I'd hate to see such a valuable comrade squashed on the rocks down below, understand?' I nodded yes. And that was it. As far as I can remember, that was it. I can't guarantee it, but perhaps Miranda added, 'This is very important, comrade. Very important.'"

Xerxes shouted Maria's name and, turning back to Molina, said, "I haven't had lunch yet, have you? Care to join me?" But he didn't even wait for a reply. When the maid entered, he ordered "Russian lunch for two."

Russian lunch? Without really knowing why, those sorrowful parakeets from Vista Chinesa still echoing in his head, Molina imagined something repulsive along the lines of herring, pickled onions, rye bread. But it was after three o'clock, and all he'd had for lunch was a hot ham-and-cheese sandwich from a deli. He told the old man he would be delighted to join him.

"Great," said Xerxes. "We'll celebrate my marriage."

"Your what?"

"After Miranda threatened to kill me in his classy way, one week went by, a little over a week, and I was married. It was simple. One day she knocked on my door, a bundle of clothes over her shoulder, and I brought her inside. I had no choice. It was a good thing I earned enough wages to rent something better than the room in the boarding house where I had been living. Two days later we moved to a comfortable little house in a workers' village in Lins. I was living like a married man, I mean; back then the most commonly heard term was 'shacked up.' In communist ethics it made no difference."

Molina tried to process the new information and was just starting to formulate the questions he wanted to ask about the woman and Miranda's role in the swiftness of that marriage when everything went off the rails altogether. Maria entered with the lunch tray, carrying an overflowing jar of bluish-black caviar beside a basket of round slices of toast and a bottle of vodka in a fat bucket of ice. Two tall, slim drinking glasses, also chilled, and sparkling silverware completed the arrangement. It looked like something out of an upscale restaurant, not Maria's home cooking. It was incongruous, but Molina was hungry. *I need to ask Xerxes for his doctor's phone number,* he thought, before they launched into an orgy of sturgeon roe and shots of icy Russian vodka. Soon the room was spinning. He rested his head against the back of the couch and looked at Xerxes. Was the old man, who'd had just as much to eat and drink as him, drunk too? It didn't look like it. Under these conditions, however, Molina didn't know if he was in the best position to judge.

5

—

On April 20, 1940, a Saturday, Rio de Janeiro newspaper A Noite *published the best interview Miranda ever gave about his life. Brought down to Rio from the prison on Fernando de Noronha in order to testify at the National Security Tribunal about Elza, the former secretary of the PCB had already fallen from grace in communist circles. But this was the first time that, in a hand-written note scrawled at the reporter's request, Miranda officially announced—or at least made public—his break with the party. He wrote, dating his statement April 21, 1940, that upon learning of the murder of Elvira Cupello Calônio, whom he referred to as his companion, he'd decided to forever sever all ties that linked him to the Brazilian Communist Party. A major factor in this decision was that the perpetrators of the crime were leading members of the party.*

Interestingly, the note was dated the day following its publication, suggesting a case of journalistic premonition.

Even better than the note, of scant significance at the time, was what Miranda told the reporter—unfortunately anonymous, as was common back then—about his relationship with Elza. I found nothing, either in the press or in books, that even comes close to this interview in A Noite *as far as shedding light on the intimate history shared by those two. Seeking out the "human side" in the news as a way of grabbing the reader by the emotional collar—something that today sits so firmly in Journalism 101 that it has already begun to tire—still seemed like some sort of accident in 1940. Elza garnered countless headlines in every paper as the helpless victim of "Brazil's most heinous crime," in* A Noite's *very own words. Naturally, the longer that note was sustained, the less human she seemed. She played a role: the victim. She wasn't really a person. No one thought to look for her relatives or acquaintances to find out what she really was like, if she got sad on rainy days, how long she'd played with dolls, if she preferred Errol Flynn or Clark Gable. No one knew anything about her as an individual.*

The only person to get close to this was the nameless reporter from A Noite, *to whom we owe a great debt for unearthing a valuable romantic fact about the two: Elza called Antônio "Tonico" and Miranda called Elvira "Vira."*

The former secretary-general of the PCB says that he first met Elza when she was a girl, "thirteen or fourteen years old," at her family's home in Sorocaba, "on Rua Bela de São João." He would show up there to attend to party affairs every now and then, dealing with her communist brothers. Back then the Cupello Calônio residence was, according to Miranda's description, a place of great hardship—though nothing that deviated dramatically from what most people in that social class dealt with regularly. Her parents, from Naples, Francisco and Emilia Luiza, were dead. Out of sixteen children, only nine were still living. Two of little Elza's sisters had "died of consumption, exhausted from work," according to the interview. Since then it had been up to her, though still a child, to run the household. What else could she do? Her other siblings were men, and household work was beneath them.

When the reporter asked Miranda about how his relationship with Elza solidified, he says that neither of them saw it coming. She heard everything Miranda discussed with her brothers but she never joined the party. One day they both simply realized that in one another's company there was a "great intimacy and understanding" between them. Miranda also says he recognized that the girl "needed stability," which was something he thought he could provide her. Finally, one day Miranda announced to her brothers that he and Elza shared strong feelings for each other and they would live together as husband and wife.

At no point did the reporter mention the age difference between the two, which is not surprising. Under the microscope of contemporary cultural mores, Miranda might seem like a Brazilian Humbert Humbert, but in the unwritten playbook of local customs in the '30s it was perfectly legitimate and even commonplace for a man in his thirties to be bagging a girl half his age—provided of course that he married her, which the communist leader swore he would do at the end of January 1936. The only reason he didn't, he insists in the interview, was "because I was arrested a few days prior."

The interview, which was that issue's feature story, was not just about the ill-starred love affair between Antônio Maciel Bonfim and Elvira Cupello Calônio. Miranda—presented as a "'bureaucratic' kind of man who cared about the cleanliness of his nails and who did not cross his legs, so his pants wouldn't lose their crease"—says that he joined the PCB after discovering that the "revolutionaries" of 1930 weren't "as radical as he expected." Substantiating his fame as a braggart, he claims he was not afraid of suffering the same punishment laid on Elza.

The most telling part, however, is when Miranda talks about his dead girlfriend. According to him, Elza was illiterate when he met her but learned to read in three weeks—one can imagine with what level of proficiency. She was, according to the interview, deeply intelligent, acutely aware, and eager to learn, absorbing everything presented to her. During her eight days of imprisonment, she was able to make a memorable impression on the other prisoners, including the communist militant Maria Werneck.

Fortunately, we do not have to rely only on the interview on this matter. Werneck's memoir, Sala 4—the name of the famous women's political prison in Rio de Janeiro that housed Olga Benário, Sabo Ewert, Eugênia Moreyra, Nise da Silveira, and Beatriz Bandeira, among others—discusses Elza. To Werneck's eyes, she did not look older than sixteen. She was always in good spirits and talked too much, showing no discretion whatsoever. Once Elza reminded Werneck of the time Elza had asked for money to print pamphlets. Laughing, Elza admitted that the money was really for buying a bathrobe for herself.

The girl Werneck described is vivacious, yes, but is also nearly a moron, or a little girl trapped in a teenager's body. Vladimir Sacchetta, a researcher with vast experience in the history of the Brazilian left, told me a story relayed to him by his father, Hermínio, the communist leader from São Paulo who was expelled from the PCB in the tumultuous purge of 1937/1938, accused of being a Trotskyist before going on to found a truly Trotskyist party. Apparently, Elza used to attend party leadership meetings, dragged along by her important boyfriend, and sit in a corner of the room playing with dolls as her sweetheart had serious debates with other bearded men on matters beyond her comprehension.

This Elza might be just another character from the Sacchetta family folklore. To my disappointment, as the scene would have added a pitiful but invaluable element to the story, no one else was able to confirm what Vladimir told me. Sara Becker, one of the few people still alive who had direct contact with Elza and the only one with whom I spoke, said she thought it highly unlikely that Elza's behavior had been so infantile.

Still, Werneck comes close to this when she refers to Miranda's girlfriend as acting childish, recounting a story Elza told her about telling a man named Serafim that she knew Werneck. Serafim was with the Central Police and was a notorious torturer. When Werneck demanded to know more about what Elza talked about with him, all Elza did was laugh.

Too bad Maria Werneck's testimony is marred by her insistence on a matter that, if it ever made sense, it certainly didn't when her book was published in 1988:

The Elza Fernandes case had several versions: she was killed by comrades who were afraid she was being followed and helping the police, or the police murdered her. How can you reach a conclusion?

Well, by reaching it, that's how.

After the meal, Xerxes opened the small wooden box that rested on the table beside him and took out two Cohiba cigars. Molina was no longer surprised. If there was still some remnant of that elderly man, more dead than alive, who had greeted him hours ago, the blue smoke that filled the room hid it well.

They smoked in silence for some time, until Molina, happily puffed up on alcohol and tobacco, said, "You owe me some explanations, you know. This woman who just appeared out of nowhere, what's that all about? You can't just throw in a huge non sequitur like that! I've got a book to write. Let's not forget my name is on the line here."

The old man slapped his right hand against the arm of his chair three times as if announcing the end of recess. "My wife, right. The day we met. For that we must go back in time a bit, but it will be worth it. It was a monumental day, my baptism by fire. If you were worried about ending up with having a mushy, saccharine story on your hands, a love story, my friend, here's a little testosterone and blood in roughly equal amounts. You should like it. Something manly finally," said Xerxes, grinning broadly, in a way that made him look just like a skull. "Maybe you've heard of the battle in October 1934 when the communists stopped an Integralist fascist rally in São Paulo. You've heard vaguely about it? Because it was something epic, my boy. All premeditated, very ably organized. That rally was billed as the biggest of all, a show of force to shake up the country. Integralism was at its height around here, a big bully with strength and arrogance that mirrored both the international blossoming of Nazi fascism and Vargas's tolerance for the movement. They knew it had begun that way in Italy and Germany, with brutality in the streets to shut up the government. If the tactic had worked in Europe, why wouldn't it work in Brazil? It was for all these reasons, as well as a jumble of old feelings of personal revenge, sore old wounds—it was for all these things and many others that the party militants mobilized on the eve of that rally.

"Actually, they weren't just from the party. I heard there had been a lot of fighting in the meetings, a lot of rows, that sometimes it seemed like our greatest enemies were right there on the left and not on the right. But in the end we were able to organize something together. That was the first time something like that had been possible, that sort of unity. Perhaps the only time. Communists, anarchists, Trotskyists—everybody was there. Every newspaper from every group had put out the call, and it was answered strongly. Let me tell you, it was a thing of beauty. It was my first important assignment in the PCB. Remember, this was shortly after I had been officially accepted. I had already met Elza at Antônio's house; she was already visiting me in my dreams, like a child succubus. But it was all still in the beginning; the kisses in the park would come later. Right at the beginning, I still could have turned back. But who wanted to go back?

"On a Saturday night I caught the train to São Paulo with three other comrades—Guarani and two others whose names I don't even remember. We got off at Luz Station on Sunday morning, the Sunday of the rally, together with people who had come from all over—from Santos, from the South, from Rio, from Minas Gerais. Longshoremen the size of those socialist-realist statues stood alongside civil servants with Coke-bottle glasses and all the muscles of a praying mantis. There was a bit of everything. At the station we already started to feel the mood. It was a nice day, and since we had a few hours to kill before the rally I proposed a walk around the city, which I didn't know. But Guarani said the plan was to go straight to the house of one of our comrades, a printer named Enzo, who lived in Brás. There would be a gathering with some comrades there, and we could get a free lunch before heading out in a larger group to Praça da Sé.

"We arrived before ten o'clock in the morning, and the house was already full. It was a modest home, white with yellow windows but with a spacious backyard with a few trees, some long wooden benches under grapevines, birdcages. Enzo, an Italian man with a stern face and thick mustache, greeted us somewhat dryly, but the hospitality was more than guaranteed by his wife, a very friendly, smiling lady. She came out from the kitchen, wearing a dirty apron, to let us know the menu was pasta with *polpettone*. I remember that like it was yesterday's lunch. In the yard we joined a group of what already must have been twenty people, everyone drinking wine. Enzo had two daughters, Francesca and Gina, pronounced *all'italiana*. These two goddesses, a Sophia Loren and a Gina Lollobrigida, were cheerfully milling about in their bare feet, going from group to group with big wine bottles, filling glasses, making jokes, laughing for everyone. *This place is heaven*, I remember thinking as Guarani nudged me to go easy on the booze. 'This isn't a party,' he said. 'Leave the partying for after the work is done.' The work was giving a beating to the Integralists. I must admit I did not follow Guarani's advice to the letter and was light-headed when we left Enzo's house, headed to war. Gina and Francesca also went. This had me worried when we approached our meeting point, at Largo de São Bento. We were being watched from a distance by battalions of police on horseback, and I started to see people with brass knuckles, clubs in hand, others carrying books by Lenin, various communist, and workers' newspapers rolled into tubes like flyswatters. But most were empty-handed, eyes gleaming with confidence, and nothing more. Did they need anything else? I understood then that no one was concerned about details like physical strength or experience in street skirmishes. There were a lot of women around, even children. It was a civic celebration. I lost sight of Gina and Francesca, but I relaxed. An absolutely irresponsible, delicious frisson coursed through the antifascist ranks: the time had come to settle the score with the scum. We tasted blood; my head was spinning, and I think that wasn't just because of the wine. If Hitler and Mussolini were beyond the reach of our sticks and stones, Plínio Salgado and his green-shirted minions weren't.

I followed the commands of comrades I didn't know; it was all a mess of people and rallying cries, and I couldn't see Guarani anymore or anyone else I knew. But I knew it only seemed chaotic. The military strategy had been plotted by João Cabanas and Roberto Sisson. Those fellows were experts. There were assembly points at Largo João Meneses, in the courtyard of the Convento do Carmo, at Praça Ramos de Azevedo. Are you familiar with downtown São Paulo? They say the green-chicken march stretched a mile long from Brigadeiro Luís Antônio Avenue, something like eight thousand people. I don't know if that is true. All I know is, arriving at the square, with women and children opening the march, green Integralist flags waving, that river of green began to be squeezed on both sides by red cliffs. If there were eight thousand of them, how many were we? That's when the taunting and abuse began. You heard 'Die!' over here, 'Viva!' over there. Some of the more riled-up ones had already started slapping around folks. All of a sudden we heard shots, but it was impossible to know where they came from. Feeling safe with the police protection, hundreds of men, an abundance of firemen, cavalrymen, and armed police officers the likes of which I'd never seen before, the Integralist orators began speaking on the cathedral steps under deafening boos. Plínio Salgado, who was no dummy, didn't show up. He stayed with his tail between his legs at the party headquarters. It was impossible to hear anything. I started to sweat profusely in that pressure cooker; the salt got into my eyes, blurring everything. Suddenly, very clearly as if from heaven, there was a piercing and unmistakable sound that until then I had only heard in war movies: a spray of machine-gun fire. Instinctively, I turned around and was going to run away, but I was saved from shame by an old woman with a black shawl on her shoulders and a grim Sicilian face, who at that moment looked to me like Death in the flesh. She grabbed me by the arm and said, 'Courage, young man.' Embarrassed, I mumbled, 'I just need to go to the bathroom.' 'I know,' replied the old woman, 'you're already shitting yourself.' I tried to salvage my honor with a snort but endeavored to quickly escape from the witch's grip. In any event, I didn't run away; my cowardly impulse had passed. I walked with studied slowness to the right, toward a denser group, where at that moment atop a crate a man had begun to improvise a small parallel rally. I recognized the guy from pictures in the papers I'd read at my uncle's house. It was Edgard Leuenroth, the great anarchist leader. I hung around, applauding everything he said, as if I were applauding my own past. I realized that similar small rallies were popping up elsewhere in the square. Suddenly, the gunfire erupted once and for all.

"No one ever found out who started it. Bullets whizzed by, people were running in all directions, and guns went pop-pop-pop. I ran for shelter behind a tree, and on the way I saw the Sicilian-looking old woman standing motionless in her place, planted there in her black shoes. She was the only person standing in the middle of that maelstrom of people, like she was the very axis of the wheel of insanity that had formed in Praça da Sé. People were falling down all over the place. I don't know if they had been hit or if they had stumbled, but either way they were being trampled by the others. There were cries of pain, howls of panic, contradictory orders—"This way," "Keep calm," "Up that way, now," "Help!" Suddenly, a disoriented kid in a green shirt passed in front of me and without thinking I punched him right on the nose. He fell to his knees and started to cry like a baby, blood gushing. 'Well done, comrade.' I felt pats on my back when I finally reached the tree I had kept in the crosshairs. There was a sharp pain in my hand.

"The shots had become more scattered; the frenzy started to settle. Someone shouted that the Integralists were retreating, and it was true. The square was expelling streams of green from every pore, a beautiful sight. Some ripped off their shirts as they ran, trying to rid themselves of that incriminating color, and euphoric comrades gathered these vile wares and held them up like trophies, yelling, 'Victory! Victory!'

"It was a victory. I had no doubt about it. That jokester, the Baron of Itararé, later said about the flight of those green chickens that an Integralist doesn't run, he flies. There was a truckload of injuries on both sides, half a dozen dead, including a communist, but it was clearly a crushing victory, and it was ours. I went out walking through the square amid the people on the ground. I recall all the abandoned hats. People were embracing one another with tears in their eyes, and it was as if I had stepped on a carpet suspended in the air. Have you ever felt that? It was as if I were standing right there and simultaneously reading about it in a history book from the future, a future that, because of that Sunday, would be a better future. This feeling of being present in the moment history happens is quite rare and often illusory, pure self-deception, but that was not the case this time. The war I had just taken part in really did enter the history books. They called it the Battle of Praça da Sé.

"That intoxicating sense of unity with fellow leftist forces didn't last more than a few hours. Before my right hand had stopped throbbing, each group was already trying to claim responsibility for what had happened, the decisive role in the victory, as they do to this day. We didn't learn much—we never did. But in any case, that unity existed for one day, for half a day, and many respected theorists later said it was that very moment that contained the rising tide of Integralism, when their arrow started pointing downward and Brazil escaped becoming a fascist country. I don't know about that. Perhaps. What I do know is it still fills me with adrenaline just thinking about it. At that moment in the middle of that square, I looked around and had a revelation: I was inside my country, and my country was inside the world, like Russian nesting dolls. We were all contemporaries, and we were all players acting out a single story, even with millions, billions, of characters, a single play. There was none of this business of structural backwardness, underdevelopment, imbalance between the center and the periphery, out-of-place ideas, cultural servitude—none of that. The global machine was gigantic but monolithic. Terrible but breathtaking. I don't know quite how to explain it. I never managed to feel that again, and I bet few Brazilians in their right mind are able to. Yet it was not false.

"That night there was a party in Enzo's backyard. Guarani and the other comrades from Rio didn't go. They had to catch the train back to get to work the next morning. Since I was not expected back at *Jornal do Commercio* until Monday evening, I decided to sleep over in São Paulo, enjoy the party, and drink that wine I had been advised to go easy on at lunch. Enzo's wife asked her husband and said I could spend the night in the little spare room they had in the yard. Actually, it was a storage shed with a tin roof, cluttered with junk, tools, a wheelbarrow, bags of provisions. It was cramped, dusty, uncomfortable, but I wasn't too picky. The excitement of a heroic day still burned in everyone's eyes, flushed faces, ferocious laughter, a crazed joy. We ate the leftovers from lunch, drank what was left in the bottles. Francesca and Gina's hopping and parading about among the diners, filling empty glasses, was even more lovely than it had been that morning. Someone pulled out an accordion, and there was dancing and singing until late:

Una mattina mi son svegliato,
o bella, ciao! bella, ciao! bella, ciao, ciao, ciao!
Una mattina mi son svegliato
e ho trovato l'invasor!

"I went to sleep on my makeshift bed of burlap sacks after midnight, when the last guest said good night.

"I woke up with someone on top of me. It was completely dark. '*Shh.*' I felt a woman's breath on my face. A tongue in my mouth. Fingers skillfully unbuttoning my shirt. Teeth on my chest. Lips on my belly. I couldn't rule out the chances of it being a dream, but it was becoming increasingly unlikely. My eyes adjusted to the darkness and I recognized Gina. I thought about telling her I was a virgin, that she please excuse my clumsiness. But I said nothing. Squatting down, she pulled her nightgown over her head in a single motion and brought our bodies together as she sat down with amazing ease, like we had done it a million times before. Before she left, Gina put her mouth to my ear and said quietly, firmly, 'This never happened, okay? *Never* happened.' Only then, in my stupor, did I understand I wouldn't have to marry her and move to São Paulo.

"I lay there half-naked, eyes wide open in the dark, unable to sleep. My heart was pounding, and I felt like laughing like a madman, doing backflips out into the yard, and shouting to the neighbors that yes, this place really *was* heaven. At the same time there was another side of me that couldn't breathe and was shaking with fear, thinking what Enzo would do to me if he found out. A quick and merciful death? Mutilation and slow agony? As I tried to decide which of the alternatives the evil-looking Italian with a Stalin mustache would lean toward, the storage room door opened again, revealing a dark figure against the blue-black night. I froze. Enzo? A 'shh' made me melt with relief. I whispered, 'Gina?'

"It was Francesca."

Xerxes ended his story and sat staring at Molina behind the smoke of his cigar, with an expression that mingled defiance, mockery, curiosity, pride. Nostrils flared, he stroked the cane obscenely with his free hand, like he was masturbating it, subtly massaging the handle. Molina didn't know what to say. The story of Xerxes losing his virginity to two Italian goddesses on the same night, a Sophia Loren and a Gina Lollobrigida—it was *too* good, too romantic. It occurred to him that those actresses were still children back then, if they had even been born yet. Was the old man making it up? For one dizzying moment, plied with vodka and smoke, he thought Xerxes was fantasizing, not just about Gina and Francesca but everything. Everything he was saying—one long, unending lie made up of smaller lies chained together. But why?

The idea was a bottomless black hole. He tried to put it out of his mind.

"Wow," he said.

The old man sniggered, like he was clearing his throat. "Wow is right. Very well put. The expressiveness of your generation never ceases to amaze me."

Molina allowed the irony to pass. For some reason, the story was beginning to seem less far-fetched. "Do you think they knew about one another?"

"That's the question I spent the rest of the night asking myself. Because of course I didn't sleep any more after that. Afraid of Enzo, I got up with the first rooster crow and disappeared; it was still pitch-black out. I kept thinking that crazy Luiz had been right! Marxism-Leninism really did hold the key to capturing the female citadel. As for one sister knowing or not about the other, you know the answer I came to? Of course they knew about each other. The timing was too perfect. They slept in the same room; they must have tossed a coin to see who would go first. They were accomplices; their shared crime made snitching impossible. It wasn't the first time they had done it. The only virgin in that story was me. My first impression was right on the mark. Enzo's house was, without a doubt, heaven on earth. In the classless society we were fighting for, all houses would be like that."

Xerxes's smile was so blissful that Molina felt a pang of envy. He didn't have any stories like that in his life. Nothing close. "Extraordinary."

Xerxes nodded in agreement. They sat like that for some time, two males dumbfounded by the outpourings of women who were probably dead, until the old man resumed his musings. "Now that you've met Gina, you'll understand why I had to take her in when she knocked on my door, bag in hand, in those first few days of 1935, thrown out of the house by the fellow with the mustache. Gina never told me exactly what her father found out or how, and I didn't even ask. Better not to know now that for all intents and purposes she was my wife, a good and honest wife who cooked for me every day, kissed me on the lips with abandon, gave me warm footbaths when I caught a chill on those cold early mornings working, mended my socks and underwear, and still found a way to earn a bit of change as a washerwoman. I didn't need, didn't want, to know anything more. All I know is Francesca was kicked out along with her, and she went to look up an old boyfriend who lived in Barra Funda. Maybe they also flipped a coin on that."

The old man licked his drooping lips, his little green eyes dancing from one side to the other in a way Molina found unpleasant, somewhat manic, and carefully put down the stump of his cigar in the opal ashtray on the coffee table. Molina had already done the same with his.

"But there's one detail I didn't tell you," Xerxes continued with new intensity. "You'll have to rewind the film a bit. Imagine that the green chickens have already run off and I'm still standing in the middle of Praça da Sé in a trance, looking around like I was already expecting to see the cover of the history book in which it all would be written hanging in the air right there. Suddenly, who do I see?"

It wasn't a question that expected a reply.

"My brother. My Integralist brother."

Like these words were a password, the air in Xerxes's living room, thick with smoke and memories, exploded into a whirlwind raised on the flapping of a thousand wings, like a flock of invisible and silent birds taking flight all at once. Stunned, Molina looked around. Shelves filled with books and photographs, tarnished knickknacks on side tables, ashtray, the frayed Persian rug, everything was in its place. Whatever had just happened there—and he had no doubt something did happen—it was not a phenomenon of the physical world.

"Huh?" Molina said.

"You didn't ask me about my brother? Well, I'll tell you about my brother. Believe it or not, back then he was an Integralist. It was only later that he joined the party, when I was expelled from it. Esau and Jacob all right. Twin antagonists, a story as old as humanity. I'm not sure if they're worth a dime, these theories that say animosity in the dispute for vital space originates inside the womb. The idea seems simplistic, simpleminded even, but why not? Those who believe in past lives go even further. All I know is that for my brother, a repentant Integralist, to join the PCB, I had to leave in the Trotskyist purge of 1938, the same that expelled Sacchetta, whom Jorge Amado called Saquila in his trilogy *The Bowels of Liberty*. But that's for another day. For now it's enough to say I had to be expelled from the party for my brother to enter. Just for you to see how far two little ones can go with the little kicking war inside a mother's belly. My brother wasn't wearing a green shirt that day. It was his luck. Or his cowardice. I don't know. He tried to sneak out of the square, picked up a red bandanna left behind on the ground, and wedged it in his jacket pocket. Without thinking about what I was doing, I ran over to him and planted myself right in front of him. Pedro was whiter than paper."

"Pedro? Your brother's name was Pedro?"

Xerxes deflected the intrusion with a swat in the air. "Name, alias, what does it matter? Like I was saying, he was livid. We stood there a good while in silence, one in front of the other, like in a mirror. Even our clothes were similar. Our hats were identical. In my brother's eyes, apart from the surprise at finding me there, I saw fear. Fear that I would reveal him as an Integralist to the leftist crowd, who by that point had taken the four corners of the square. Minutes went by. It felt like hours. Then I gave him a strong hug and told him to get out of there. He disappeared."

6

—

The definitive proof of Miranda's treachery? I first heard about this compromising letter, signed by the former secretary-general of the PCB and addressed to Rio's chief of police, Captain Filinto Müller, in a November 1985 interview in Afinal *magazine with journalist Fernando Morais, author of* Olga. *Morais said that, unfortunately, by the time he laid hands on this essential piece of evidence proving that Miranda had become a police informant, it was too late. His hugely successful fictionalized account of the tragic life of Olga Benário was already on the shelves.*

Only those who have already gone looking for a needle in the haystacks of old records can imagine my excitement to stumble upon these two typewritten pages among Filinto Müller's personal papers, archived in the Getúlio Vargas Foundation Center for Research and Documentation in Contemporary History. Even if the tone and wording of the letter were not as eloquent as they are, with flourishes of bootlicking and indignity, it would merit attention because it has not been discussed at length in any other book I have been able to locate.

Written in Rio de Janeiro and dated July 11, 1942, the long letter opens and closes with birthday wishes for the honorable chief of police. Miranda commends him for his tenacious efforts to protect

Brazil in a struggle of great political and historical import. What Miranda goes on to offer, identifying himself as a doctor in such matters, are remedies to the "illness" plaguing the country and the methods by which to best administer treatment. It is quite the birthday present.

Miranda feels no need to elaborate on his role in the party, insinuating that his early work has made him famous. But then he mentions Elza's death, saying that she died in his place, and as a result he has now committed himself to fighting against the tide of bolshevism, the same as Müller. The reason for this, as exemplified in Elza's murder, is that the communists have organized anew, sensing an important final battle, and in doing so have become even more polarizing than in the past. Miranda praises Müller and President Vargas for "saving" Brazil from the communists in 1937 and insists that if similar great actions are not taken, then there will be no way to save the homeland.

Miranda then goes on to explain the party weaknesses, countering the perception that communism has become a chaos of splintered factions. Not true, he writes, calling into question the notion that the "Marxist hydra is showing another head." Nothing has changed about Marxist intentions or methodology. To this end, Miranda tells Müller that any footholds the party has found in Brazil in the past are the result of being able to count on the support of naïve government members. But the party knows it cannot count on Müller or President Vargas, he writes, and this is its greatest vulnerability.

It is as if Miranda writes all of this to Müller to tell him that the government has nothing to worry about this time around. Furthermore, Miranda cites his life's experiences as reasons for his shifting convictions, pledging to stand in solidarity with the government "in the fight against bolshevism."

I was convinced that this letter proved beyond a reasonable doubt that Miranda had switched sides until I showed a copy to

Sara Becker. With nearly eight decades of communist militancy pre-
served in her ninety-three-year-old brain, which seemed more lucid
than my own, the widow of journalist Murilo Melo kindly invited
me for an enjoyable conversation in her apartment in São Paulo
that lasted hours. To Becker I owe, besides contact with someone who
had personally met Elza, the perspicacity to dismantle the farce of
"Miranda's letter to Müller."

She doubted the letter as soon as I mentioned it and before she
had even looked at it. That surprised me. Since Becker is a Joseph
Stalin sympathizer to this day, I vaguely expected her to readily
accept any evidence against Miranda without batting an eye, as so
many of her comrades had done throughout history. I was wrong.
There was no hatred for Miranda in her memories. He was, according to her, a good man. His breaking from the party seemed very
unfortunate to her, but a natural, human reaction after what they
did to Elza, the girl he loved. I began to think I had a lot to learn
from Becker.

But I didn't think I would learn that much. She read the letter, issuing expressions of disbelief the entire time, and when she
arrived at the signature she said, "His name wasn't Antônio Maciel
do Bonfim. There was no 'do.'" Stunned, I grabbed the pages she
handed back to me. It was true. At the bottom of the second page
the name of the author had been typewritten and, immediately
below it, signed in pen—the only part of the letter not typed. In both
places there was the unwarranted addition of "do." Sara smiled at
my astonishment, rhetorically asking, "Who gets their own name
wrong? The letter is a fake. You must be very careful with police
archives."

After this discovery, it was relatively easy to assemble a seemingly consistent thesis about what could have motivated Filinto
Müller to falsify, or have falsified, a letter from Miranda. At that
time—July 11, 1942—Rio's chief of police was fighting for his

political survival with all his strength. One week earlier he had been involved in a violent clash with the ambassador Vasco Leitão da Cunha, who was temporarily in charge of the Department of Justice. Müller had denied permission for a large pro-Allies march scheduled in Rio for July 4. Leitão da Cunha went over Müller's head and gave the green light for the rally.

The fight was far from trivial. With World War II raging, and under President Getúlio Vargas's prolonged indecision—winking to one side one moment, to the other the next—the leadership of the Estado Novo was engaged in a game of tug-of-war that was decisive for the country's future. On one hand, Chancellor Oswaldo Aranha's supporters, which included Leitão da Cunha, were pulling Brazil to the side of the Allies; on the other, the minister of war, Eurico Gaspar Dutra, was leading a group that wanted to see Vargas arm in arm with Hitler and Mussolini—after all, they had considerable similarities of style.

On the eve of the pro-Allies march, Müller went to Leitão da Cunha's office, demanding an explanation. According to some versions, he was so upset he even pulled a gun. Nonetheless, he wound up losing the battle. On July 17—just six days after the letter—he was fired by Getúlio Vargas, along with the minister of justice, Francisco Campos, and the head of the feared Department of Press and Propaganda, Lourival Fontes. The little gang of fascists had hit a low point. Approximately one month later, Brazil declared war on the Axis.

It is worth rereading the "letter from Miranda" in light of this power struggle—or fight for the Brazilian dictator's heart, as the episode might also be interpreted. This clash between Filinto and Leitão da Cunha, between those sympathetic to the Germans and those siding with the Americans within the Estado Novo, is the letter writer's pretext, with his supposed authority as a former communist in denouncing those sympathizers "who have been placed" within the government.

Too convenient, too eloquent, too timely, and too laudatory of its addressee, the "letter from Miranda" bears all the markings of a commissioned piece. Yet the possibility remains that it could have been written by a Miranda who was entirely subservient to the chief of police who had ordered him tortured, if not for the crude slipup with the incorrect signature that Sara caught. I found no record of any other document where Antônio Maciel Bonfim had signed his name this way.

From one perspective, it's a shame the letter doesn't hold up. It was perhaps the last hope to give some solidity to the soggy ground that now seems destined to remain a bog forever.

After this episode, Müller never regained the good graces of Getúlio Vargas, who obviously did not see him as the "mainstay" of the Estado Novo, as proclaimed by "Antônio Maciel do Bonfim." Even without the dictator's support, however, the former Rio de Janeiro chief of police continued his political career with voters in his home state of Mato Grosso, and he was elected senator three times. For a man who won the infamous title of Patron Saint of the Torturers of Brazil from the left, he fared rather well. He died in July 1973 as real political hotshot in the famous Orly plane crash that also killed bossa nova singer Agostinho dos Santos and socialite Regina. He was president of the National Congress and the National Renewal Alliance Party (ARENA), the ruling party in the military dictatorship. Political columnist Carlos Castello Branco gave him a more than respectful obituary in the Jornal do Brasil *newspaper, calling him a "cordial man, stern but affection-ate, a kind host." However, being the good journalist that he was, he included the caveat, "As to the degree of responsibility in the crimes committed in the shadows of the dictatorship of 1937, that is a secret buried amid the wreckage of the Boeing that crashed outside Paris."*

Miranda's level of involvement with the police was another secret that died with Müller. Unlike Müller, the former leader of the PCB fell into complete obscurity after 1942. He left jail in poor health—he'd lost a kidney from so many beatings—and struggled to find work. Journalist Edmundo Moniz, now dead, told historian Marly Vianna he had helped Miranda, getting him a job as a proof-reader for a Rio newspaper. Elza's "widower" reportedly didn't take long to return to Bahia, where he died young. No one could tell me exactly where or when. It's as if, instead of actually dying, Miranda had slowly turned into a ghost.

An entirely inappropriate ending for someone claimed by so many to have been the "backstabber," the number-one son of a bitch, etc. Is it conceivable that he was so stupid as to sell himself for nothing?

In what was possibly Miranda's final appearance, he makes a cameo in the marathon interview Carlos Lacerda granted a group of reporters from Jornal da Tarde over a period of five days in 1977, around a month before his death, and which was later transcribed into the book Depoimento. Miranda enters the picture when he introduced himself to Lacerda during a gala lunch at the Portuguese Gymnastic Club, in Rio. The interviewee doesn't give a date but recalls that he was still working as a columnist at Correio da Manhã, placing the event before 1949, the year he founded his own newspaper, Tribuna da Imprensa. The lunch was given for him by a "trade union of manufacturers or sellers of construction materials," Lacerda recalls with a certain imprecision. After "some forty speeches" at the table covered in wine and salt cod, that "skinny and weathered" man stood and said, "Our guest doesn't recognize me, but he will soon remember who I am. My name is Antônio Maciel Bonfim. I want to inform you that today I am a Roman Catholic and, as you know, I am considered a traitor by the

Communist Party, which killed my companion. I am an employee of the union."

Lacerda, a right-wing leader who had also been expelled from the party in his youth, then adds that Miranda came up at a social gathering in 1977, not too long before this interview. Lacerda emphasizes the important difference between hearing a story and reading it, recollecting how a friendly young girl employed by the Getúlio Vargas Foundation had heard, when a student at Catholic University, that Miranda had switched sides in exchange for the job of librarian for the police department. As Lacerda is quick to point out, calling out this story as a lie, the police department never had a library. He goes on to explain how no man turns his back on a lifetime of idealism for something as worthless as a paltry job. So, he concludes, "It's a detail, but an important one. The way you can twist an entire story. A whole story is only valid if it is told with all its merits, negative and positive."

In Molina's eyes, the monument was a freak, an eyesore. A head with elephantiasis; an abscess about to pop in the square's face; a long, jarring fart at a gala dinner. The bust of Getúlio Vargas seemed to contrast with the sleek white lines of the Hotel Glória, its illustrious neighbor, like a greenish-black turd in a fine porcelain toilet. The three tons of bronze were a nightmare, an abomination, an antitribute, a mockery that wasn't supposed to be there. Oversized in every way, especially in relation to the trees and the flower-beds around it, the bust intended to announce to passersby the Vargas Memorial, inviting them to come inside, worked in reverse: it was a scarecrow, something that after seeing for the first time and being surprised, you learned to avoid at all costs. Better to turn your gaze on anything else—a garbage can, a mangy dog, a festering wound on the leg of a homeless man sleeping on the Aterro footbridge up ahead—anything but that. On the mornings he awoke in a good mood, Molina was able to see the humor in that iniquity, thinking it was like Vargas trying to compensate in posterity for his diminutive physical size—and his big rear end, as writer Antônio Carlos Villaça once noted. But he didn't always feel so kind. On bad days the bust in front of Camila's house became the ultimate emblem of all the disproportions, deformities, and ugliness that human intervention had inflicted on the natural landscape of what had once been the most beautiful city in the world.

When he awoke that morning, Camila had already left for class. Laura was also not around. In the kitchen he found Luz in just her panties and a T-shirt, eating Frosted Flakes standing up.

"Good morning, Mo."

It disturbed him. It was the first time she'd called him that. He turned his back and mumbled, "Good morning," but so quietly she probably didn't even hear him. He left the house in a rush, on an empty stomach, pursued by the sight of Luz's adolescent thighs. They were spectacular. He went down in the elevator with accordion doors that reminded him of *Rosemary's Baby*. Blinded by the sun when he got outside, he crossed the lane toward the square and walked robotically toward the Vargas monument like someone yielding to the perverse attraction of an abyss. From close up, it was even more frightening. A dog peeing on its marble-covered base—a massive nine-foot-tall block— looked at Molina and decided to ignore him. He finished his business, then left quietly, heading in the direction of Radio Globo. Molina was alone, just him and the old dictator. It occurred to him then that, without the madness of Prestes, of Miranda, of the Comintern, this artifact wouldn't exist. Under normal conditions, Vargas wouldn't have lasted long. He grabbed on to the opportunity the insurgents of 1935 had given him, galvanizing public opinion against the Red Peril. Of course it worked—when had the Brazilian public ever remained indifferent to good patriotic fanfare? A few months after the failed uprising on Praia Vermelha and at the aviation school, the country's then capital was still under siege and a climate of terror. The main leaders of the revolt were in prison, the Knight of Hope at their fore. His wife, a German Jew named Olga Benário, would soon be served up on a platter, pregnant, to the Gestapo. A sad story; very sad story. Why, then, did Molina get so much pleasure out of diving into it?

After a black coffee and a grilled ham-and-cheese at the nearest greasy spoon, he walked to the National Library. It was a ten-minute trip between tree-lined flowerbeds in the shade of the Nossa Senhora da Glória do Outeiro church on one side, and the Museum of Modern Art on the other. It would make for a pleasant stroll if it didn't involve crossing high-speed lanes choked by huge vehicles driven by those with no respect whatsoever for traffic lights, not to mention the nooks occupied by packs of homeless people with watery eyes—minefields of human, canine, feline, and pigeon excrement, deep trenches, overflowing manholes, trash everywhere. Around the Passeio Público, the landscape changed thanks to bevies of street vendors, with their tarps and stalls dripping with products from Abibas, Sonya, Raph Luren, Panafonic, Tosheeba, Niake, Eve San Loran, Shanel, S'Puma, ReyBon, Padra, Gutchi—merchandise from another world, a parallel capitalist dimension inside the mirror.

Molina made his way back in the early evening after a few watered-down beers in Amarelinho Bar. He was distracted by the ill-digested memories of his day's research but realized that this time the walk was even more depressing. When the cold streetlights came on, the packs of homeless turned into circus rings of transvestites, and prudence advocated swapping the waterfront with the inside path, between the worm-eaten buildings on Rua da Lapa, a dirtier and uglier route, without the Museum of Modern Art, the church farther away, but also busier and better lit. But in spite of all the ills of his dying city, which had never failed to depress him, Molina returned lighter, a man with a twinkle in his eye and a spring in his step, a mood he hadn't felt in a long time.

Realizing that the National Library was approximately the same distance from Camila's house as Xerxes's apartment, just in the opposite direction, was also a source of delight. He liked that symmetry, which seemed to obey some higher purpose, drawing for his footsteps a radius of walks to make peace with the city.

For seven weeks Molina met regularly with Xerxes in his Flamengo apartment, always in the afternoon—Mondays, Wednesdays, and Fridays. The duration of the interviews— or monologues, as Laura had made a point of highlighting—varied from a minimum of two hours to a maximum of six, practically nonstop. The pace was dictated by the old man's fluctuating disposition. At some of these meetings, Molina didn't see Maria. In her place, a professional nurse named Katharina, dressed in white from head to toe, took care of Xerxes. She was a tall and strong woman of an indeterminate age, with blond hair and pretty features, though exaggeratedly proper. She never smiled and just called Xerxes "Doctor." Discreet, she spent most of the time in one of the bedrooms, away from the chatter her patient poured out in the living room. She never asked him to rest. Molina found this surprising, as sometimes even he, who wasn't there to care for Xerxes's health, was alarmed by the energy the old man invested in reconstructing the past. It was an admirable show but a bit scary. Sitting stiffly in his wingback chair, cane resting on his knees, the man gushed a continuous stream of words, giving himself over to the task with disciplined abandon. As if there were no future, thought Molina. Only later did he realize that, for Xerxes, there really wasn't.

His tactic was to let the old man talk, asking minimal questions and offering few asides. In a small notebook he kept open on his lap, he jotted down under the day's date the topics of conversation and occasionally a more complete remark made by Xerxes or a thought that corresponded to whatever it was Xerxes was saying. Read later, these lists of words in deplorable ink-smeared handwriting looked like the gibberish of a madman. One of them said, "Wednesday, 5/14, Comintern, congress, frenzy, spies who came in from the cold, X: comedy of errors, conspiracy or picnic?, revolutionary Lampião, hahaha." Yet Molina trusted those curlicues to guide him in the ocean of digital recordings he was accumulating.

On days she was there, Katharina interrupted their work from time to time, but only long enough to take her patient's blood pressure or temperature, make him swallow some pills, and give injections. Molina didn't know exactly what was wrong with Xerxes. The day he asked him, the old man laughed and said at ninety-four it would be easier and less time-consuming to tell him what *wasn't* wrong with him. "Old age is murder, son," he decreed. No matter the nature of his clinical condition, it wasn't serious enough to keep him from smoking a Cohiba every evening and, when he seemed particularly satisfied with the day's work, ordering a repeat of his Russian meal from Maria. Molina was reassured by these excesses, figuring a person's health couldn't be failing that badly, at that age, if he splashed about the way he did. Until the day he saw Katharina respond to Xerxes's request and serve him a shot of vodka. The absurdity of the scene—the nurse extending the frosty shot glass with the same air of professional severity as she dispensed medication—astounded Molina. From that moment he began to see what until then he had interpreted as evidence of the old man's good health the other way round: libertinism that compassion, having lost its last hope, grants those whose days are numbered.

Xerxes didn't always keep the conversation focused on the events that led to the insurrection of 1935 and his participation in them, his primary concerns. There were days when the man's chatter rambled as he lost himself at forks in the road and down blind alleys. Molina did nothing to bring him back to the main road. On the contrary, he enjoyed these diversions. They humanized the old man, as if scratching doodles on the solemn bronze statue—History Incarnate—that Molina had erected for him in his mind. One afternoon Molina made an unassuming comment about a certain television actress whom he had seen in the street on the way there and how she looked less beautiful in real life. Xerxes remarked that they didn't make actors like they used to. He wound up talking for almost an hour about the Rio theater scene in the 1930s and '40s, actors like Procópio Ferreira and Oscarito, Dulcina de Moraes and Eva Todor, with a familiarity that surprised Molina. It was the first time the man ever revealed his fondness for the theater, a pastime for uppity middle-class snobs—highbrow petty bourgeoisie, as perhaps he himself had said, people he didn't hang out with. When Molina expressed astonishment, the old man became uncomfortable, as if he'd been caught in a foible.

"Pedro was the one who got mixed up in the theater, not me," he said. "My brother had talent, you know? If you're curious, you can still see him in a bit role with Carmen Miranda in a picture called *A Voz do Carnaval*. He told me he had two or three lines. It's a shame they were all cut in the editing room. Pedro enters a mute and leaves silent, but"—and Xerxes started laughing—"what beautiful body language! His political militancy got in the way of his career. He even worked on *Vestido de Noiva*, directed by Ziembinski, but back then, in the early '40s, he was more involved than ever with the party. He always gave priority to his cell meetings. This resulted in him sometimes arriving late to rehearsals or not showing up at all. He ended up fighting with that Polish queer and resigned from the company one month after opening night. It was sad. Today he would be immortalized in the history of Brazilian performing arts."

Molina, who had never heard Xerxes speak about his brother so affectionately, jotted down in his notebook, "Pedro actor, proud brother, Esau and Jacob???" Maybe less than the old man had implied at the start.

Near the end of May, halfway through the fifth week of interviews with Xerxes, Camila announced she was going to spend a few days in Caxias do Sul, where Cobra, from São Paulo, had sought refuge from the persecution she suffered from her family and the police for her sexually subversive ideas.

"It's too bad you can't come with me, Mo."

They were having dinner at Luigi's for the second time that week. Taken aback, Molina placed his fork and knife on the plate. "What about your classes?"

"Classes?" she laughed. "Who cares? It's only one week, a week or so. Did I tell you that Cobra opened a cabaret in Caxias called Royal and changed her name to Suzy? Isn't that typical?"

"What's typical?"

"Typical," Camila repeated, a hint of annoyance in her voice. "Patriarchal society forced the poor thing to fall right into the whole whore stereotype. There was no room for the middle ground she sought, true female autonomy. You're either a saint or a whore. Cobra, of course, would rather be a whore. She always spoke of prostitutes with pity, but with a lot of understanding as well."

"But did she really become one?"

"I dunno. Close to it, managing whores. That's what I want to find out about in Caxias."

Molina knew he should be happy with the news, the announcement that Camila, the most serious girl of her generation, was taking off to the far reaches of Brazil, propelled by her passion for the crazy feminist she had chosen as her thesis topic. But he couldn't feel happy. It seemed unfair to him that his girlfriend was going away right at that moment, just when he really needed her. He thought about the nights he'd spend alone at the apartment on Botafogo Beach, running Xerxes's chatter on a perpetual loop in his head without being able to discuss it with anyone. He felt helpless, and the more helpless he felt, the more he realized how ridiculous he was being.

The awareness of being more dependent on Camila than he'd like to admit united with the shame he felt from his own selfishness, ruining the meal. He had deliberately cultivated this dependence. In the early days it was something enjoyable, like the natural extension of his determination to burn bridges with the world of mediocrity—with the world itself. The bet he had made with himself six or seven months earlier, ditching a declining career in journalism to be an author, a professional of the written word, had resulted in great failure. Even at the worst moments, however, Molina always believed that not all would be lost as long as his girl stayed by his side, for obscure reasons that went well beyond the dubious agenda he'd drafted for his life. Drinking wine and stirring around on the plate the rest of a risotto he no longer felt like eating, he conceived a grim thought: there was nothing more, no one else, anywhere. He was dangling in the void by his dick.

Mine, mine, mine—the old mantra started to echo in his head as if triggered automatically in situations of panic. On second thought, what was one week apart? His bad mood seemed laughably irrational. To hide it, he said, stumbling over his words, "That's great, baby. It's too bad I can't leave Xerxes and go with you. Won't it be cold up there in the mountains? Wouldn't it be nice to sleep all snuggled up, light a fire? Better not to think about it. But I wonder what you'll be able to find out about Ercília in Caxias after all this time."

Camila shrugged. "Who knows? Maybe I'll find my own Xerxes. Worst-case scenario"—she smiled, big, black eyes sparkling—"I come back full of stuff to write a nice study in Virtual History."

"Do you want dessert?" said Molina. "Want to share a crème brûlée with me?"

Distracted by his premature longing and his embarrassment to discover it affected him so much, he didn't pay any attention to what Camila had said nonchalantly until later on, when he recalled the scene. It seemed deliberate: Virtual History. What did she mean, Virtual History? It wasn't a fluke, a made-up expression. It was a real concept. But he only found out as he was about to fall asleep in his girlfriend's bed, the fish tank's blue light imbuing the room with a dreamlike atmosphere.

Camila whispered, "Mo."

He cracked his eyelids. Camila was lying on her stomach, propped up on her elbows, facing the headboard, far from sleep.

"I'm taking an extracurricular course with a guy who's a genius. You know him."

"I know him?"

"He told me you two studied together."

"We studied together?"

"His name's Franco."

That's how Molina found himself, a thousand miles away from Camila, making a call to Zé, who he hadn't seen in over two months. Zé was Molina's only friend from the old days, the last one to defy the misanthropic maxim that, after the age of thirty, making new friends is impossible and losing the old ones, inevitable. The old ones die, fall away, escape down the drain, and in their place new ones don't sprout up. Molina called the phenomenon "emotional baldness." On his way to the meeting he'd set up with Zé in Serafim, the dive bar in Laranjeiras where they used to drink, he caught himself humming an old hit by Léo Jaime:

You've got all kinds of friends
and I've just got Zé.

Though they had been friends since college, Zé was, when Molina really thought about it, a boring guy. He had two very distinct sides, and Molina didn't feel comfortable with either of them. Government employee, married for fifteen years to Tiz, four children, early member and devoted supporter of the Workers' Party, Zé was one of those millions of citizens above reproach who drowned the slightest possibility of existential unease in the well of conventionality that their lives, digging in a little deeper each day, became. The problem was Zé's other side wasn't any better. After a dozen or so beers, Molina's only friend began to turn into a mushy, tedious wild-eyed guy. A few ticks of aggressiveness would emerge from his flat surface, along with some equally exaggerated recesses of tenderness. At these times, this craziness made Zé perilous, ridiculous company, capable, in under five minutes, of making a crude pass at the old woman at the next table, insulting the waiter for a poorly poured beer, falling to his knees on the dirty floor to beg for forgiveness to the same waiter, breaking down in tears, and yelling to Molina in between sobs, "I love you, Molina! I love this guuuuuy!"

But that would come later. When Molina arrived at the tiled bar on Rua Alice that night, Zé was still nursing his first beer. A skinny guy with a drawn face, he looked more serious than usual. When they spoke on the phone, he had voiced his reservations about his friend's new job, asking predictable questions: "Why write about Elza Fernandes? Who's interested in telling that story?" Surely, he was ready to go deeper into the subject now, Molina thought, preparing to defend himself against a half-dozen leftist clichés tossed at him at his expense. But he'd called Zé for other reasons. As soon as a drink was in front of him, Molina jumped right into it, dispensing with the usual niceties. "Do you believe Franco was reincarnated?"

Taken aback, Zé sat there stunned for a few moments, but he soon shifted his body to swing back. Two decades of ping-pong had made the friends good at this. "In whose skin this time?"

"A little genius."

"You don't say!"

"A guru in something called Virtual History."

"Which happens to be . . . ?"

"As far as I understand, it was Franco who invented the thing. Quackery, of course, but there are a lot of young historians, slack-jawed students, in his classes. Waiting list to register and all that. Virtual History argues that likelihood, and not the truth, is the litmus test for historical accounts. So, the historian isn't only able to make up things; he must— he needs to fill in gaps, cheerfully assuming his inner novelist. Only then will the work make sense on human terms, instead of a cold report on dead materials."

"Cold and dead," said Zé. "That's a good description of your sex life after fifteen years of marriage. But this, um, theory isn't new, is it? Weren't they saying something similar in '68?"

"When did Franco ever do anything original, Zé?"

Molina then realized that there was a sort of poetic justice or metalinguistic meaning in all this talk of Virtual History. From the very beginning, almost everything about Franco was made up. Not by Franco himself, which would turn him into an absolute phony, but by all those around him—artists and *artistas* from the Rio alternative circuit in the '80s, when he built a brilliant reputation as a writer, performance poet, entertainer, cultural agitator, video maker, and who knows what else, without actually being any of those things. Why would he, if he was the guy all well-bred young girls were keen to give it up for when they wanted to seem cool? The guest no party would be complete without? All this was encouraged by the opportune gaps Franco had scattered throughout his history, eventually encompassing almost the entire thing. He wasn't a total phony; he was a bit of a phony. He defended himself by asking who among us wasn't a phony to some extent.

He'd come from the suburb of Marechal Hermes, that much was known—he hadn't been able to erase that far back. But he'd erased the clueless suburban nerd he had been during his first month at the School of Communications of the Federal University of Rio de Janeiro: sheepish, ugly, short-sleeved dress shirt, grandpa sandals. A virgin too of course. Only child of a sad, sinking middle-class family, his father an office janitor at the Treasury Department, whose only activity akin to leisure was to set a chair on the sidewalk and spend his weekend drinking beer and reading one paperback Western after another. No wonder his mother, a homemaker, suffered from chronic depression.

Interestingly, those cheap little books, with titles like *Stagecoach to Hell* and *Justice is Done with Lead*, were Franco's springboard for the metamorphosis witnessed by the campus on Praia Vermelha filled with old-growth trees. He had to lean on something, and his father's Westerns played that role. The rest of his origins he methodically stamped out; he even burnt photos. Later on, as his fame started to spread, the blanks would be filled in by the far-fetched rumors that on his way from Marechal Hermes to Zona Sul he'd made a stopover in London to become friends with Joe Strummer, gone to Recife to teach a young Chico Science how to play the triangle, had gone on epic binges with rocker Itamar Assumpção at the Lira Paulista Theater, and posed nude for an AIDS-awareness campaign that the government shelved because it was too racy. Somehow all of these myths and badly told stories clung magically to the suburban kid and transformed him into Franco, a larger-than-life character. But it all started with *Ten Desperados and One Bullet*.

On those sluggish suburban weekends when he was a kid, Franco had also read his share of books like *Parade of Corpses, Occupation: Murder, Fatal Canyon, Crimson Dust*. They were right there, forgotten about as soon as his father finished them, leaving them in the kitchen, in the bathroom, wherever. The cartoonish covers were signed with unlikely names like Randy Dollars, Rip Comanche, and Lucky Barr. The title and the pseudonym came to him simultaneously: *Ten Desperados and One Bullet*, by Frank Franco. He wrote the story that first month, wearing grandpa sandals, on Praia Vermelha beach, secretly devising the butterfly—a manly one, if those exist—that his incredibly caterpillar-like self would become. It was a classic Western, with a wandering hero, a beautiful widow on a ranch, lusted after by bandits, an old, complacent, and corrupt sheriff, a good Indian, and all those Colt revolvers spitting fire under the blistering sun.

A Western that was so tidy, leaving no loose ends, but with some extra sprinkles of glorified violence and expressionist sex to improve sales that the publisher, a dump located up in Estácio, was happy to publish it for free. How could they know that Frank Franco had twisted Texas history to mirror campus life at a Rio university?

The widow, Mel Beaver, was a carbon copy of Melanie, the student-body president, whom a gang of shady bearded guys was trying to take down. The cowardly sheriff was a dead ringer for the director. Staff, professors, and students gave life to the supporting characters. The Indian, Limp Feather, was inspired by Molina, the author's best friend at the time. Unsurprisingly, the hero got muddled with Franco.

> *"Mr. Hardon, I don't know how to thank you," Mel Beaver said, taking a step toward Frank.*
>
> *The hero hesitated. He wasn't accustomed to lily-white, sweet-smelling women fresh out of the bath, so different from the creatures of hardened skin and eyes he mated with like an animal and then left behind as he continued his Old West wanderings. He looked deeply into the widow's green eyes as if staring down his opponent in a duel under the sun. He said nothing.*
>
> *"At least," Mel Beaver continued, smiling a grin of perfect teeth and taking another step, "show me the blessed gun that saved my life and my ranch, Mr. Hardon."*
>
> *"You can call me Frank."*
>
> *"All right, Frank. Is it a long barrel?"*

It was all the rage. In no time, the twenty copies Franco had bought from the publisher at a discount to distribute on campus had changed hands several times and turned into collector's items. The sandals were swapped for All

Star high-tops, the dress shirt for Ramones T-shirts; his hair grew and stood on end. The hoop earring would come later. Melanie liked the tribute so much that she did to the author exactly what Mel Beaver did to Frank Hardon. His virginity lost thanks to literature, Franco became a monster who treated the witnesses of his prepop existence with brutal hostility—Molina and Zé were first in line.

"Someone ought to expose that clown," said Zé, lifting his empty glass to order another beer. Molina silently agreed. It was better not to tell his friend that Camila— *mine, mine, mine*—was among the suckers who thought Franco was a genius. Then, pausing halfway as he lifted his glass to his lips, a thought came over him and was gone like the glimmer a fish makes in the water before it swims away. Molina spent the rest of the night with the vague feeling he had taken a half step back and was finally seeing, beyond just the horseshoe, a piece of the leg on that horse from the epic mural. Was it a dun horse? But everything was drowned in beer. Just a bit more and Zé would be doing his whole declaration-of-love number, and the next morning Molina wouldn't remember a thing.

7

—

The organization called Communist International, or Comintern, was founded in 1919 by Vladimir Lenin, with the mission of reproducing around the globe—which at that time meant Europe—the socialist experiment of seizing power that had been so successful on the steppes two years earlier. Besides being loyal to the old Marxist idea of the international vocation of the workers' revolution, the Leninist plan to export bolshevik technology had been trying to build above (or dig below) nationalities an escape route to lead the country out of its isolation at that time, when it was subjected to a harsh trade embargo by European powers.

In practice, Comintern was an arm of the Soviet Union's Communist Party, but national parties that had started sprouting around the world like mushrooms following World War I were officially treated as "sections." Perhaps the modern business-franchise model isn't a bad metaphor: the parties needed to satisfy a list of twenty-one requirements to be accepted into the organization; they had relative autonomy and accountability, received political and ideological guidelines, occasionally even welcomed an intervener disguised as an advisor, and periodically sent representatives to Moscow for congresses or study trips.

The proliferation of communist parties was truly exuberant in those years—and perhaps would have happened inevitably thanks to the success of the Russian Revolution. As a sponsor of revolutions, however, Comintern reaped one fiasco after another: Germany, Hungary, Austria, China. By the end it hadn't embarked on a single successful insurrection.

When its creator died, Joseph Stalin, the godfather who took his place, tried to undermine the powers of the organization, though it would only be abolished in 1943. The idea of internationalism was falling out of favor, identified with the thinking of Leon Trotsky, Stalin's adversary within the party. It didn't take long before Trotsky was purged. Cast as the bogeyman of the new order, Trotsky was labeled as a sellout, lackey of the bourgeoisie, despicable traitor to the working class, and other such kindnesses.

The decline in Comintern's prestige on the Soviet stage is reflected in the number of international congresses it organized: one per year while Lenin was alive, from 1919 to 1923, and just two over the following two decades. Its role also changed as the Soviet Union, no longer a sniper, strengthened diplomatic and commercial ties with the states it had intended to destroy. During its final years, Comintern was just an appendix—increasingly irrelevant—to Stalin's foreign policy.

In August 1935 the seventh and final congress of the Communist International approved a line of caution and moderation, based on alliances and popular fronts. That represented a radical shift. The previous CI congress, in 1928, had banned alliances as tactics of the right and adopted an ultraleftist policy, which, by raising the social democrats—or "social fascists," as they were called—to the role of "primary enemies" of the communists, had contributed invaluably to the rise of fascism in Europe. The change came late. Too late, as they would soon see.

Too late not only in Europe, where the new form of the extreme right had taken on a vigor that only the greatest war of all time could contain, but also, in a certain way, in Brazil. When the shift *took place in the seventh congress, in August, the South American giant was already resolutely headed in the opposite direction of conciliatory times. Not only did the Comintern know about this but it supported the armed attempt to seize power in the country. Why did it do this, going against its official party line? To what extent was it actively involved in the conspiracy led by Luís Carlos Prestes, a member of its executive committee?*

Scholars have always been divided by these questions, in a sort of soccer match between old rivals that is still waiting for the final whistle to blow—today it's experiencing a sort of drawn-out overtime. Eudocio Ravines, a former Peruvian communist who published his famous memoir after breaking with the cause, disdainfully stated that in 1935 Brazil was the Comintern's "lab rat."

Brazilian thinking on the insurrection can be divided into two main sides that, if we decided to be completely unoriginal, we could call "left" and "right." On one side are the historians who downplay the Comintern's role in the events of 1935. To them the coup attempt was exclusively Brazil's doing, the final hiccup in the same Tenentism junior officer uprisings that, begun in 1922 and growing in the epic Coluna Prestes movement, had helped bring Getúlio Vargas to power in 1930. A movement, therefore, that could only be understood within that historical moment, when young Brazilian military officers, inspired by positivist ideas, thought it was great to take up arms every few years to save the homeland from the yoke of the old oligarchies.

Across the battlefield—and the transformation from sports metaphor into war might be forced, but not much—stand the historians who point to the abundant documentary evidence of Soviet involvement to paint the uprising in the exciting colors of international intrigue. This version recognizes that, although the anticommunist propaganda of the Vargas government had trumpeted to the point of exhaustion issues such as the "Moscow Gold" and taken maximum political advantage of the experienced international agents sent to Brazil—well, none of that was a lie, was it?

Coincidence or not, the books that most completely embody these two views were released almost simultaneously in the last decade of the twentieth century. Revolucionários de 1935, *published in 1992 by communist historian Marly Vianna, looks to dry out Moscow's role in the episode. This line, which Prestes himself defended until his death at ninety-two, in 1990, was second nature for the communists for decades. This was understandable. How can you admit, without provoking a serious diplomatic incident, that the Soviet government had an official arm for meddling in the domestic affairs of other countries? Impossible. So, according to this point of view, the uprising was merely a direct consequence of the fact that Vargas had criminalized, in July of that year, the mass movement represented by the National Liberation Alliance (ANL), a broad front that prominently included the PCB, with Prestes as honorary president. Of the "democratic, anti-imperialist, and anti-fascist" aspirations of the banned ANL, the armed uprising would have thus become the ultimate—and, admittedly, pathetic and desperate—escape valve.*

Ignoring Moscow's influence in the episode became harder when, in 1993, one year after the release of Revolucionários de 1935, *came* Camaradas, *by journalist William Waack. Based on extensive unpublished documentation consulted by the then reporter for the* Estado de São Paulo *newspaper in the archives of the former Soviet Union, opened for the first time, Waack's book tells the same story from a different angle: a tragicomedy of errors on a global scale.*

Both books seemed fine to me. Each has its weaknesses: Vianna's insistence on downplaying the international dimensions of the events of 1935; Waack's tendency to cartoonishly magnify negative psychological traits of those involved in the conspiracy. But overall, both appear to be well-researched, well-argued works and deaf to the crudest catchphrases hammered over time by the left and the right: that the insurgents killed fellow soldiers in their sleep, for example; or that in Luís Carlos Prestes, to use the memorable words of Jorge Amado in his book O Cavaleiro da Esperança, *"the negative sides never arose."*

This is not to deny the existence of real differences between the points of view roughly divided here into two groups. Or to reduce their differences, which are innumerable, to a simple dichotomy. Absolutely not. I prefer to let the differences face off, the sources explain themselves, the interpretations collide and cancel one another out or enrich each other, as appropriate. The bibliography at the end of this book may provide some routes for those who wish to go deeper into these issues. Obscure elements abound in the 1935 adventure, enough to, paraphrasing James Joyce, keep historians occupied for three hundred years. Most don't even fit in this book. But the more I read about the matter, the more it seemed imperative to me to not unconditionally adopt either of the conflicting points of view.

I believe that such a decision has to do with the fall of the Wall rather than with being on the fence. Because after that it would be a shame to not go beyond mere polarization to recognize what, being obvious, may displease everyone: the inexperienced military insur-rection of 1935 was a belated episode of the Tenentism uprisings, without ceasing to also be one of Comintern's projects. No surprise. To believe 1935 only makes sense when viewed in profile—or from the front or above—is to reduce the debate to obsolete, Manichean pairs, relics from the Cold War: "bourgeois history" against "par-tisan history"; "sellouts" versus "ideologues"; "winners' discourse" versus "Stalinist falsification"—to name a few of the charming terms each side spent decades doling out to their opponents.

In this rivalry of polarization, intelligence is cast as a mere extra in an old movie with an out of sync soundtrack, screening for eternity in an empty theater. And if that decaying oldness is called for what it is and the empty theater appears in the movie, it might actually be interesting. A novel has these advantages.

In the late 1920s, Luís Carlos Prestes, a young military genius from southern Brazil who garnered international fame as leader of the legendary Coluna Prestes social rebel movement (1925–1927), precursor to Mao Zedong's Long March, was a leader in search of a cause. Exiled since he had entrenched himself with the undefeated Coluna in Bolivia, on the eve of the so-called 1930 Revolution he had two secret meetings with Getúlio Vargas in Porto Alegre. Social scientist Paulo Sérgio Pinheiro considers this bipartisan meeting "the most fascinating in the entire history of the Republic of Brazil" and notes that the two men—destined to be mortal enemies in 1935 and allies in 1945—"met up to not meet up." The captain of the Coluna received $30,000 from Vargas, in theory to buy weapons and militarily control the movement that would bring down the Old Republic. He never did any of this, but he didn't return the money. He kept it for a revolution he believed in.

In 1931 Prestes converted to communism and, accompanied by his mother and four sisters, moved to the Soviet Union. Four years later, after he landed clandestinely in Brazil in April 1935, he faced the peculiar situation of being directly affiliated with the Comintern—whose executive committee he would soon join—without actually belonging to the PCB, which still regarded him with suspicion. He traveled on a passport in the name of Antônio Villar, Portuguese merchant, and in the company of Olga Benário, a secret service agent of the Red Army ordered to protect him.

It was time for the small fortune Prestes had received from Vargas, which he'd donated to the Comintern, to begin its return journey. It wouldn't take long for it to earn the media nickname "Moscow Gold," even though it came from Brazil via Moscow.

In Rio, Prestes and Olga were joined by other agents sent by the Comintern. The most senior included the German Arthur Ewert, best known as Harry Berger, and Ukrainian Pavel Stuchevski, who for decades of Brazilian history was only known by his cover as the Belgian Leon Jules Vallée. The former was Prestes's political advisor and the latter, a career bureaucrat, was in charge of conspiracy finances. Both brought their wives, which, when you consider that Prestes and Olga had fallen in love on their way to Brazil, made the command of the movement of '35 quite a lively couples' enterprise. The three couples were also joined by the German Franz Paul Gruber—an explosives expert actually named Jonny de Graaf, but this would only be discovered decades later—and his stunning blond girlfriend, also German, the young Lena. As well, of course, as the couple from Buenos Aires, Rodolfo Ghioldi, head of the Argentine Communist Party, and Carmen.

There were also a few bachelors among the agents sent by Communist International to help Prestes bring down Vargas: the American Victor Allan Baron, in charge of setting up a clandestine radio station to communicate with Moscow, and the Italian Amleto Locatelli. But the couples influenced the group so much that it is understandable, though unforgivable, that Miranda involved Elza in something that she, unlike the rest of the other halves in question, didn't come close to understanding. He didn't want to go down in the history of the conspiracy as the third wheel.

"The year 1935 started out very well for me," said Xerxes, "and there was nothing to indicate it would end in disgrace. It was the first properly adult year of my life. Gina devoted herself to me and to the house, like I was a prince.

I gained weight, grew a nice mustache; they gave me a raise at the *Jornal do Commercio*. Soon we decided to have a child, and each day we repeated our, let's say, attempts to do so. Sometimes three, four times a day."

The old man smiled proudly. Molina absentmindedly smiled back. He felt somewhat alien to the conversation, as if he were hearing Xerxes's words muffled from behind a plate of glass. He'd hardly slept the night before—maybe one or two hours, no more, just before daybreak. Right before going to bed, the phone call from Camila—rushed, hazy, the line full of static—had left him in a strange state of anxiety. When he realized sleep wouldn't be coming anytime soon, he tried to circumvent his impatience in front of the TV, watching for the thousandth time *The Twilight Zone* DVDs he'd bought a few years earlier on Amazon. It didn't work. At dawn, resting his head on the pillow again, he would close his eyes and see what was left of the beautiful robot wife, her face destroyed by a cold, casual gunshot, wires shooting out.

"Wake up!" he wrote in his notebook. Xerxes was talking about sex.

"Nearly always during the daytime," he said, "because I used to work nights, late into the night. I only woke up in time for lunch. But afternoons were ours. Back then I was sure my wife would make me forget about Elza."

Katharina came out with an enormous syringe and, without saying a word, kneeled beside the wingback chair and started to administer a yellow injection in Xerxes's left arm.

"I liked to take Gina by surprise when she was busy with pots and pans in the kitchen," the old man went ahead, with perfect indifference to the injection, "or sweeping the house, washing clothes behind the house. She pretended to protest, called me a sex maniac, but in the end she'd die laughing. She was always ready to go. We earned a bit of a reputation in the neighborhood, but that didn't bother me one bit. Not even the fact that Gina wasn't getting pregnant bothered me. We were good as we were, I thought. What's the rush?"

Molina looked at the Teutonic profile of the nurse kneeled on the Persian rug, her milky skin streaked with blue veins, searching for a sign of blushing from her patient's conversation. He found none. Katharina pulled out the needle, pressed a cotton ball against the prick, stood up with the ease of an athlete, and left the scene. But her intervention had helped Molina to wake up.

"I didn't yet know it at that point," said Xerxes, "but there was another sort of gestation under way, the gestation of the much-dreamed-of Brazilian revolution. Actually, almost no one knew; there were just half a dozen in the leadership. As someone more inured to the cynical view of the world could recall, the leadership of the Vargas government also knew. But that's another story. At that strange meeting at the Vista Chinesa overlook, Miranda had thrown out a few hints, speaking in grandiose terms of the future of the communist cause in Brazil. A future he painted as immediate, concrete, at hand. We were prerevolutionary. I remember he used the expression 'prerevolutionary state.' But it never crossed my mind that his words could be anything more than bullshit, leader's rhetoric, from the same family as bloody redemption, workers' militias, bourgeoisie crushed by the wheels of history—I was pretty fed up with that contrived and exalted language. It was routine, but woe to him who trusted in it. There wasn't a single rally that didn't include identical types of bombastic language, at times on the lips of some pale fellows who would obviously pass out if they had to kill a cockroach. In a nutshell, I didn't take Miranda seriously. Of course, knowing what we know today, I was right. The problem is that a lot of people *did* take Miranda seriously, starting with Manuilsky, who said something that must have been the pride of the PCB at the time. After he heard Miranda's famous delusional explanation, the big bully of the International grinned and said our party showed such strength, was so advanced in the mass movement, that it was an example to be followed by the Argentine communists. Imagine—all of a sudden we were an example for our neighbor's party, which was older than ours and so well respected that the South American headquarters of the Comintern was located in Buenos Aires. It was a shocking statement really. But did I say that at the time almost no one knew about the plans for the insurrection? No, that's wrong. *Until the end* almost no one knew, only the highest-ranking leaders. It's hard to understand what they intended with that. Some type of spontaneous combustion of the masses once the fuse was lit? Maybe. Prestes relied on his mystique with the militants, that's for sure. He believed his legendary name would be enough to rouse barracks around the country. The PCB relied on God knows what. It seems his delusional reports, after they were swallowed whole by the professional revolutionaries in Moscow, didn't seem so delusional after all. Looking for affirmation, to show the masters that it was all grown up, the PCB lied its head off, said exactly what the masters wanted to hear. When these lies came back in the form of a plan of action, it was as if they were true. Madness. One thing fueled the other—an important Brazilian scholar says this. Help me out, boy. Who was it?"

Molina was startled. "Who said what?" Xerxes waited, his eyes glued on him. Another test, and right on a day he'd slept so badly. "It was, it was . . ." he faltered, scribbling willy-nilly in his notebook. The names of the authors he'd been reading nonstop were dancing around in his head—Hélio Dulles Pinheiro Werneck Sodré Silva Vinhas Dainis Caballero. Molina felt all the anguish of Burgess Meredith's character in his favorite *Twilight Zone* episode, the lone survivor of a nuclear war who has all the time in the world to read the books he'd always wanted to, but out of the blue he drops his Coke-bottle glasses on the ground and hears the lenses smash.

When he got tired of waiting, Xerxes said, "I think it was Paulo Sérgio Pinheiro."

"I think so too," Molina agreed, feeling more down than usual.

"Well, it doesn't matter. I think it was Pinheiro who said that the center of global communism was thrilled by the secondhand version of its own ideas. Closed loop, you understand? I'm pretty sure it was Professor Marly who had a famous definition for the environment in which the conspirators were moving: 'a demented world.' It's interesting to notice, son, how such a controversial story, which to this day makes academics come to blows, has at least one point everyone agrees on: it was outright madness. Even Prestes, after he got old, recognized this in a way. Sincere self-criticism was never his strong point, but, recalling the uprising, Prestes placed the blame for every fiasco on poor Miranda, and the most he could come up with for a defense of the movement was saying it was honest. Isn't that funny?

An *honest* movement. It never had any real chance at victory;
it was limited to just three or four barracks, was ignored by
the people, fortified Vargas, cleared the way for the Estado
Novo dictatorship, landed thousands of people in jail, filled
the torture chambers, destroyed the party, and gave the
right a supply of legends and bogeymen large enough to last
until the end of the century. But, oh, it was honest beyond
question!"

Xerxes had a wild look in his eye. Molina was still tor-
menting himself for having done so poorly on the test.

"I found the first hint of that demented world by
chance. In May 1935 I bumped into Josias in a pool hall on
Tiradentes Square, a nice merchant marine, strong, brown-
skinned man from Bahia, built like a horse but with the face
and mannerisms of a big kid. A really nice, really decent guy.
More than a comrade, he was also my friend. He used to go
to samba circles with me in Saúde. It had been a couple
of months since I'd last seen Josias, so I asked where he'd
been. At first he didn't want to say. I had to buy a half-dozen
beers before I could get him to open up. Then Josias whispered in my ear that the party had sent him to make contact
with Lampião, the great revolutionary leader of the peasants in the Northeast. Apparently, they chose Josias because
he was from Bahia, and someone thought it would be easier
for someone like him to get on with Lampião than for, say,
someone from Maranhão, a couple states over. I never quite
understood that. Lampião was from Pernambuco, and there
was no one on hand in Rio who was from Pernambuco. The
envoy had to come from here; the mission was too important
to be delegated. Anyway, Josias—back then some knew him
as Hélio—he went up there, all important, to meet Brazil's
most legendary bandit. In his bag, besides a change of

clothes, he carried a leather binder stuffed with pamphlets about the revolution of 1917, the Communist International, the PCB, the peasants' struggle around the world, the guerrillas in the field, the subsequent formation of the Soviets—basically Marxism and Leninism 101 for outlaw bandits. It didn't take long for Josias to make contact with Lampião by way of a sympathetic farmer—someone's uncle, I don't remember exactly who. It was the sort of thing where one day Josias left a message, and the next day came the reply: yes. They would meet right there on that farm. Lampião set the day and time. Josias told me that on the appointed day the sun was hot enough to melt a statue of Lenin. His little joke isn't so funny anymore after the statues of Lenin really did melt, but at the time it was a good one. So standing there by a gelding was my friend, waiting where they told him the captain would appear. Two goons whom the farmer friend had borrowed were squatting around him, one on either side, each holding a sort of small carbine in his lap. Josias stood the whole time, sweating buckets, smelling his own stink. It was the stench of sweat, sure, but it was more than that. Fear? Lampião's messenger showed up first. He was a stocky guy, thick skin, full head of hair. Absolutely frightening, at least Josias thought so, and Josias was no sissy. From up on his horse, the man chatted with the silent henchmen. Well, chatting in a manner of speaking. The bandit grunted. The henchmen barely moved their heads. The bandit spit to the side. One of the henchmen spit to the side. The other henchman spit straight ahead. Josias tried to spit, but his mouth was dry.

"The *cangaceiro* bandit glared at the city slicker, who by now was feeling absurd, with his urban shoes, a pair of sensible black work shoes but urbane and ridiculous in this setting. The bandit spent some time looking at Josias. Josias held his gaze, until my friend couldn't stand it anymore and said, trying to instill a tone of cheerful confidence in his voice, 'Hello, comrade!' The *cangaceiro* burst into laughter, a long, mocking howl. All of a sudden he whistled through his teeth, louder than a bellbird, and Josias couldn't help but wince a bit. He pressed the briefcase against his chest, seeking strength in the revolutionary spirit inside.

"The gang came bellowing out of nowhere, and suddenly twenty or so horse-riding bandits were upon him. There were no women. Maria Bonita, Lampião's famous girlfriend, didn't make an appearance. 'Who's the communist?' The pleasant and clear voice sprang from the middle of the bunch. It was Lampião.

"After dismounting, Lampião came over to shake his hand, a firm handshake, and pulled aside Josias. They stood chatting for a few minutes, or rather, only Josias was talking. He talked without stopping out of pure nervousness, explaining the proposed alliance between communism and *cangaço* bandits, using all of the jargon of those days.

"He opened the leather briefcase and started taking out mimeographed papers as he talked about class enemies, feudalism, landowners, and the devils of industry. Lampião was just listening, a smirk glued across his face. When Josias stopped talking, Lampião looked him right in the eyes and said, 'You see those chaps over there?' and pointed to his gang, who had dismounted and formed a circle around the two henchmen from the farm. 'They're just nuts to lop off your noggin. I told 'em to wait till I heard what you had to say. Now that you laid out all this hogwash, you know what? I didn't understand a thing.' The smile was still glued on his face. 'Now, what do you say? I let 'em cut off your head or not?' Josias told me his legs buckled right then, and he couldn't think straight. All he could manage was to stammer, 'But captain, but captain . . .' Then Lampião cackled, gave him a friendly slap on the back. 'You get on outta here real fast,' he said, 'and never come back. You can leave the briefcase; I liked all those papers. Paper's damn hard to come by out here.' Josias obeyed him. He left so afraid that it was only the next day, on his way back to Rio, that he understood Lampião's, shall we say, sanitary plans for those papers."

Molina laughed, definitively awake, and jotted down: "toilet paper."

"Did you like the joke?" said Xerxes with childish glee. Molina thought he would start clapping. "Want to hear another? Do you know the story of Canellas?"

"Who?"

"No, of course you don't know it. No one who's not a card-carrying communist knows the story of Canellas. But it's a stupendous story, my boy. The kind of story to make you double over in laughter, sit down on the curb, and get sick from so much hilarity. But you might also be cast into a strange, sticky depression for weeks. It depends on your state of mind, depends on the moon. I say this because both things have happened to me. I've reacted in very contradictory ways thinking about the story of Canellas."

Maria entered the room carrying a tray on which was the inlaid box that contained the Cohibas. She left it on the side table next to her boss. Molina would only register the novelty of it later, in retrospect—the maid and the nurse present on the same day. At the time he just waited for Maria to leave the scene before speaking again.

"Who is this guy?"

"Antônio Bernardo Canellas, the first delegate from the PCB at a Communist International congress. The fourth congress, in 1922. The Brazilian party had just been created by a handful of pseudointellectual craftsmen who'd graduated from anarchism, with Astrojildo Pereira leading the way. And while I'm building up the suspense"—Xerxes winked his little light green eye maliciously—"why not build it up some more? Before I tell you the story of Canellas, I'm going to let you in on what has always haunted me about this story. Something I spent my life searching, pondering, intrigued by, until finally, an old man, I came to understand it. More than an anecdote, a poignant vignette. It's as if the story of Canellas were a creation myth in negative. Brazilian communists never rid themselves of the story of Canellas. It stayed there forever, like a raven perched on the door, a book's mocking epigraph, projecting its meaning on all the history that came after. About Elza even. Or mostly. But we also don't need to be in such a hurry."

Xerxes paused. He was panting, his slender arm reaching for the glass of water on the tray brought in by Maria, beside a line of pills of various colors. Molina had seen that parade of pills before, but he'd never paid them any attention. This time, vaguely thinking it might be his last chance, he tried to remember each pill—shape, size, color—as Xerxes popped them in his mouth and swallowed with a look of disgust. He counted nine. He thought there seemed to be fewer the previous week, five or six. Could the line be growing?

"Canellas wasn't really a communist," continued the old man. "The error starts there. He wasn't in Brazil when Astrojildo and the others founded the party. He sympathized with the revolution of 1917, but that doesn't mean much. The left sympathized almost in full force—it was early yet; there was room for a certain innocence. The truth is, Canellas, a printer born in Niterói, was an anarchist down to the last strand of hair on his head. A very active anarchist. They said he was smart, witty, but also very rambunctious, self-centered, and a liar—anarchism was full of guys like this. A guy who'd founded his share of little newspapers around the country and had become friends with the people who now, coming from anarchism, had decided to sow the seeds of scientific socialism in Brazil. Canellas didn't attend any of the founding meetings of the PCB. At that time he was in Europe, apparently Paris, participating in a union activity or something like that."

Molina let himself sink into the leather couch, more satisfied than ever with his role as listener. He was just a pair of ears, and he was happy. Pairs of ears don't think about faraway girlfriends. He didn't understand where Xerxes was going with this story, but the illusion that the old communist would fill eternity with words was comforting.

"Suddenly, the newborn PCB, a babe in arms operating out of a little room in downtown Rio, received a head-turning gift—an official invitation to participate in the fourth congress of the International in Moscow. Can you imagine how happy those fellows were? Well, I can. Internationalism was everything back then. We had been given the chance to set in motion the party's recognition with the CI—as long as we weren't a section of the International, we were nothing but a joke. The problem is that the euphoria had barely settled in before we got hit with a cold shower. The trip was going to cost a fortune, the party didn't have a dime, and time was in short supply. What a shame, it seemed impossible to get to Moscow on time."

Xerxes took a longer than usual pause. Accustomed to the way the old man used his silence for a sense of drama, Molina suspected that this time he'd actually just stopped for lack of breath. But as the silence stretched, Molina became worried. What if Xerxes wasn't able to fill eternity after all?

"It was Astojildo's own idea to send Canellas." The old man's speech, as he continued, became distressed, his sentences punctuated with short, gasping breaks. "Canellas was a clever guy and was already nearby, more than halfway there. It must have seemed like a brilliant idea. How could Astrojildo ever imagine how much he would come to regret it? Canellas was a disgrace. Or a crowning achievement, depending on your point of view. He started out by fighting with the delegates from Argentina and Uruguay. Then he started sticking his oar into all the items on the agenda, even if they had no connection to Brazil and Latin America. No matter the subject, Canellas heckled, disagreed, went on tirades. Even in those pro forma votes on matters that had already been decided, done to ratify a position negotiated during high-level meetings. There was, for example, a motion to repudiate the French delegation for exhibiting traces of Freemasonry. Canellas voted against it. He found it arbitrary, decided to defend the Masons. He created a reputation. Trotsky, who was participating in the congress, gave him a nickname that stuck: 'South American Phenom!' With an exclamation mark, please."

Xerxes interrupted the story again, this time to laugh. He laughed so hard and in such an excruciating, choppy way, slapping the arm of his chair, that Molina prepared himself for one of those coughing spells that threatened to send him straight to his grave. The coughing never came, but the effort wore him out. His eyes closed, head thrown back against the chair, the old man sat motionless for some time, a rattle coming from his chest. Both Katharina and Maria appeared to see what was going on. Suddenly, without opening his eyes, he continued.

"There's no denying the guy had cheek. Democratic centralism had never been so demoralized in the history of the Soviet Union. Canellas anarchized the celebration—literally. Later on they found essays in the CI archives that he turned out there on nineteenth-century England, on the situation in Zanzibar and in South Africa, industrial decentralization, the impact of new artichoke-growing techniques on the pharmaceutical industry in Lapland. It was really something amazing. Trotsky had been right: a phenom! The result was the CI denied PCB membership. They said the Brazilian party still had too many anarchist overtones, that it could be accepted as a sympathizer at most, not as a true communist party. It was utter bedlam. When news of the disaster of the Brazilian delegation arrived back in Brazil, that began the PCB's first crisis. And the first purge. Canellas tried to defend himself in a lengthy report that would have worked better as an indictment. It was so obvious to anyone who read it just how far off he was from wrapping his head around it. To make things worse, he threw a tantrum and published the report without the party's knowledge. They wound up kicking him out, officially declaring him a traitor. Of course, wanting to be in the International's good graces, there was nothing else Astrojildo and the others could do besides disown Canellas, casting him out, getting rid of him with the highest degree of public humiliation. And they really wanted to. The PCB's membership was approved the following year."

When he finished saying this, Xerxes opened his eyes and looked at Molina. He seemed better. He played around with his cane, tapping it on the rug. Molina wrote a single word in his notebook: "Canellas."

"I don't think I understood why you consider this Canellas the raven perched on the PCB's door."

"Of course you didn't understand. Didn't I tell you that I only understood once I was old? But you'll understand when I explain."

"I can hardly wait," Molina said.

The old man cocked half a yellow-toothed smile. "Am I detecting a touch of sarcasm there?"

"Sarcasm? Of course not. Why would I be sarcastic? Just because since we started working you've treated me like a moron? Just because every day I leave here wondering why this old man hired me if he thinks I'm so stupid? No, no way. I would never dream of being ironic because of that."

Molina surprised himself. He hadn't realized that his irritation with Xerxes, like a dam filling up slowly, had reached the point of overflowing. The old man looked at him with his mouth open. *Okay,* he thought, *I lost the job.* But soon Xerxes was smiling again, shaking his head.

"The second sign that something big was under way," he said, "I only noticed in August, when they called me up to participate in an elite group that would receive training from a certain German expert. Everything was shrouded in mystery and even some pomp. The comrade who summoned me, Tenório, made me memorize a list of spots, passwords, and codes that would change each week. From these meeting points I would be taken to another place for the training, which would also never be repeated. I couldn't even tell Gina, Tenório told me very seriously. 'Of course not, comrade. I never tell my wife anything.' He said, 'Great. If you never tell her nothing, then now you've got to tell her less than nothing, tell her nothing at all. Nothing about nothing about nothing at all.' That started to scare me and I asked, 'What is this training?' 'Training in sabotage, comrade,' he whispered. 'Explosives.' Only later I learned that the German, the teacher, was Gruber."

Molina's heart thumped one hard beat. "Did you meet Gruber, sir?"

Xerxes replied with the expression of a sphinx: rigid, upturned chin, crazy eyes, his shoulders feigning disdain. It was hard to say if meeting Gruber was the highest or the lowest point of his life. "I wish I'd never met him. Gruber was a scab, a madman. A professional, for sure, a professional revolutionary, the most professional I've ever met. But a crook, a gangster. Maybe you're wanting to ask me what that 'but' is doing in the last sentence, between a revolutionary and a crook, eh? You sure you didn't think that? Well, no one knew exactly what Gruber's game was back then. No one, at least among the Brazilians, even knew his real name. We only found out much later. Franz Gruber only became Jonny de Graaf for us recently, when that kid on television got into the archives in Moscow and wrote that book. Even more recently, an American historian said the fellow was a well-traveled spy, really well traveled. Not just a double agent, Soviet and British, as everybody suspected, but a triple agent—he negotiated with the Americans later on too. That book, incidentally, hasn't even been published yet. I only know about it because I know people who read the original and told me. In any case, it makes sense. The gadget Gruber installed in Prestes's safe to destroy the conspiracy documents in case the thing was ever dropped never exploded. Folks already thought this was strange; they always thought that Gruber was suspicious. Take his connections with Filinto Müller, which everyone knew about. Müller arrested Gruber and then released him immediately. But being sure about everything, proof of his dangerous game, took a lifetime. Or many lives. One day, young man," said Xerxes smiling faintly, "you'll discover that about Brazil. It's a national trait that becomes increasingly clear over the years: everything here suffers from supernatural delays. Things take a long time, torturously long. Being young in a place like this is no joke, because being young means being in a rush, and being in a rush in Brazil is halfway to suicide. You can write that down."

Molina wrote down "supernatural delay."

"The fact is that back then, for us, Gruber was still an unknown, just a guy who'd fallen out of the sky on the occasion of a Latin American revolution, teaching the natives how to make bombs out of coconut water and macaw feathers and turn a banana into a stick of dynamite. Yet I already knew he was worthless. I knew almost without knowing, but I knew. Gruber was a big huge son of a bitch. When a guy is like that, those who coexist with him know it, feel it, have no doubt. He was a stout, short, strong German man with a perfectly forgettable face that served him well as a spy. The girlfriend he dragged with him to Brazil was a lovely little blond thing, not even twenty years old, who we just called the little German girl. She became Prestes's trusted driver. She went everywhere with him, knew every address. Only later, when the story of de Graaf came to light, did we find out that Lena had been given to him by her parents, a couple of poor souls who had the double agent as their protector. Feeling indebted to Gruber, they paid him with their daughter, if you can imagine. A daughter of that quality no less!"

Xerxes licked his droopy lips, his eyes darting. Molina had already learned to interpret those signals: it was excitement. Sexual, sensual excitement, or any shadow of that still left at his age. The old man's fingers massaged the handle of his cane.

"Ah, Lena," he moaned. "When the uprising failed and they were strangely let loose by Müller, they both fled Brazil. Everything suggests Gruber killed Lena in Buenos Aires before going on alone to Moscow, where he'd been summoned. Surely she knew too much. A disgrace. Top-quality woman, as some lucky comrades could attest, from what I've heard. Good gossip, huh? I can't swear to it. But the couple was odd. Apparently, Lena took a few spins out and about, and Gruber—well, he was awfully crazy about Elza. No, he didn't screw her. He got down on his knees for her because he was a cradle robber, a Humbert Humbert before the term was coined. But I seriously doubt he was able to get what I couldn't get. Try, boy did he try. Why would Elza show up from time to time at our secret explosives-training sessions in isolated farmhouses in the suburbs? Just to cook and wash dishes? It was kind of odd. On those occasions Elza never came to talk to me, and I still can't forgive myself for not going to talk to her. But she smiled at me from a distance. Those were the last times I saw her."

8

—

The "revolution" began with a premature ejaculation on November 23, in the 21st Hunters Battalion infantry unit in Natal, capital of the northeastern state of Rio Grande do Norte, surprising even the conspiracy leaders in Rio de Janeiro, who only learned of it from the newspapers. Rebel soldiers succeeded in taking the humble capital for four days, long enough for them to set up a "popular revolutionary government" and release one issue of the Liberdade *newspaper. If there had been any chance of catching the Vargas government by surprise, however, that opportunity was lost. The next day the 29th Hunters Battalion of Recife rose up and, from his hideout in Ipanema, Prestes began firing off little polite dispatches inviting a large number of officers, some staunchly loyalist, to take part in overthrowing the government, to be waged on such-and-such day at such-and-such time, please do not delay. In the early hours of November 27 Rio finally followed the lead of the Northeast: a few dozen soldiers under the command of Captain Agildo Barata took the 3rd Infantry Regiment, on Praia Vermelha beach, while others tried to do the same with the Military Aviation School. That was it. The government suppressed the revolt, going so far as resorting to bombers on Praia Vermelha, in time for lunch. The end.*

The crackdown that followed led to a huge number of arrests. "According to police data," says Nelson Werneck Sodré, "in December

1935 and January 1936 more than seventeen thousand people were arrested; more than twenty thousand, according to PCB data." Included in this tally were communist militants, mere sympathizers, leftists in general, liberals, and even a few instances of those "quite to the contrary." It was Getúlio Vargas's hour of reckoning with anything that smacked of opposition.

Conspiracy leadership began to unravel on December 26, when Harry Berger, an alias for Arthur Ewert, and his wife, Sabo, were arrested in their rented house on Rua Barão da Torre in Ipanema, allowing unbelievable documentation on the plot's secrets to fall into the hands of the police. Juicier still were the documents apprehended minutes later and just two blocks away on the same street, in the house Luís Carlos Prestes and Olga Benário had hastily fled. The arrest of Ewert, a German Jew, gave way for O Globo *newspaper to run off with the trophy for that period's most unfortunate headline: "Son of Israel and Agent of Moscow!"*

Hiding out with Olga in a little house on Rua Honório in Méier, Prestes wasn't arrested until March 5, 1936. The period of just over two months that separated the arrests of Ewert and the Knight of Hope contains a whole world of intense police activity, filled with triumphs and blunders. Those taken down included, among others, Rodolfo Ghioldi and his wife (both released without a scratch); Victor Allan Baron (killed by his torturers but made to look like suicide); Stuchevski and his wife (released apparently in exchange for serving as bait, but the police never saw them again); and, of course, Miranda and Elza.

Elza spent two weeks incarcerated. Released at the end of January, she was encouraged to return whenever she wished to visit her sweetheart. The party, nerves on edge, thought that was strange—with good reason. Exactly what Filinto Müller's police force intended by releasing Elza never became entirely clear. Stirring up some sort of confusion was certainly part of the plan. Maybe she could lead them to someone important or perhaps wind up a suspect in the eyes of her own comrades, triggering a new and gladly received crime. Either way, Elza seemed more useful on the outside.

After Miranda's girlfriend was released on January 27, Prestes, holed up in Méier, began a frantic exchange of letters and notes via courier with the two highest-ranking leaders of the PCB still at large: Honório de Freitas Guimarães, known as Martins, a very odd character who had studied at the traditional English boarding school Eton and was the widower of an aristocrat; and Lauro Reginaldo da Rocha, called Bangu, an exponentially mediocre man, who two years later would inherit command of the party and lead the rumored purge of São Paulo leaders accused of Trotskyism.

The police found copies of those letters in Prestes's possession when they arrested him. They documented step-by-step the events leading up to Elvira Cupello Calônio's death and ended up as centerpieces in the proceedings opened at the National Security Tribunal after her body was found in 1940.

The prevailing mood in these correspondences is one of panic and confusion. Rumors and speculation are passed on and soon debunked by contradicting claims that were no more reliable. Who was tortured? Who reported the comrades? Someone who was with Miranda in jail reports he is "all black and blue, his nose broken, and needles under his nails." Another report, attributed to a certain Mattoso, a journalist linked to the party, goes into horrible detail: "I was there with Miranda. He took an incredible beating. There are still signs of the needles on his nails. They also squeezed his balls, forming an abscess that burst. Punches in the stomach and belly until he lost consciousness for five days; three beatings like this in just one day, one after another. His nose is broken. Bruises on his eyes and body, etc., etc., etc. Infirmary, nervous system a wreck, doctor, medicines. Doing better and cheerful. Calm and self-possessed." It's difficult to reconcile this portrait with Graciliano's description of a spry, joyful Miranda, isn't it? Mattoso also states that "Elza received terrible beatings for three days. Naked, and the cops twisting her breasts. They didn't get a single word out of her. Great bravery."

So how was it possible that Elza walked out of the jail just a few days later without a single mark on her little sultry body? And what about her spreading the rumor that Berger—yes, Berger, the toughest of them all—had behaved disgracefully under torture? It was all very suspicious undoubtedly. Just like the little notes from Miranda that Elza brought to the comrades outside. The messages were apparently sincere, advice to those who remained at large, recommendations of caution, but it was puzzling. Were they falsifications? If the notes were authentic, why did the police allow them to be circulated? "Who are the authors of the letters with messages from Miranda? I don't know them. The letters appear written, or at least dictated, by the police," says Prestes.

Everyone believes that the Girl—or G, as she was referred to in these letters in which, obviously, no given names are used—is guilty to the core. Her death, euphemistically referred to as "extreme measures," is quickly decided, although at first no date was scheduled; the first note in which the attention-grabbing code word appears is dated February 3, one week after Elza's release. One single comrade, waiter José Lago Morales, firmly opposes the verdict. This only manages to get him removed from subsequent meetings.

It was immediately decided that Elza would be removed from the home of Francisco Meirelles, a former communist from a good revolutionary family, brother of Silo and Rosa, who had housed her based on ties of friendship. Better to take her to a faraway place where trusted comrades could keep an eye on her twenty-four hours a day. They chose a suburban home rented by the militant known as Gaguinho, on Rua Maria Bastos, near Camboatá Road and the Deodoro Train Station (back then the neighborhood known today as Guadalupe was called Ricardo de Albuquerque). At that point in the twentieth century, it was halfway between the city and the country. One of the notes addressed to Prestes states that when Elza arrived there she was "very nervous and scared," "afraid to drink things, eat, etc.," but she soon saw the "brotherly atmosphere" and calmed down.

In Gaguinho's house, Elza devoted herself to the household chores that were her specialty—cooking, cleaning, ironing—so much so that four years later she received a compliment from her host in his police statement. Every day Adelino Deycola dos Santos, who everyone called Tampinha, would interrogate her. Her answers were forwarded, along with the impressions and feelings of her brotherly wardens, to Luís Carlos Prestes. Everything Elza told Tampinha was regarded with immediate suspicion. Even something that was of no benefit to her under the circumstance and could only be sincere:

The girl says the beatings she received boil down to hair pulling by Romano (who grabbed it and said it looked dyed), two thwacks with a rubber baton on her back, and two on the soles of each foot, and around six slaps on the back of the neck. Apart from that she said nothing else happened, no tugging her breasts, not even the thing P told B. That stick up her vagina she said didn't happen to her . . . There are contradictions apparently about the three days of torture that Mattoso speaks of and which she denies.

Elza's firmness under pressure is evident in the reports from those critical days. Her guilt, however, was treated as a premise:

As you can see the girl continues to dwell on all this that she attributes to our dear Miranda. My duty is to break down and transmit what she's harping on, by inspiration from that source we know.

From a distance, Pavel Stuchevski, who after outwitting the police and lacking a better place to go spent time in the house where Prestes and Olga were hiding out, used his experience as a senior Soviet intelligence agent to assist Tampinha in interrogating the Girl. Forwarded to the people at Rua Maria Bastos on February 9, the questions of the Ukranian—who at the time everyone believed was Belgian—reveal one chief concern: the letters attributed to Miranda that he and Prestes deemed fakes.

What color was the envelope?
Where was the letter written (in his cell, the common room, etc.)?
In whose presence was the letter written?
She says she saw Miranda several times at the Central Police station. How many times? Where? On what floor?
What does the common room look like? The cell, the doorway?
When was she beaten? Was she undressed?

On the same day, Prestes makes it clear that he was already convinced of Elza's betrayal. Now it was just a matter of learning more about the police's methods:

She still seems to be saying only what the police taught her. It will be of great importance for us to know now the truth—that is, to get her to really say how the police prepared her, how they instructed her, what methods they used, with what resources they bought her. But all this must be obtained little by little, with a

141

lot of patience and persistence, and principally by a firm person who knows where he is going.

Perhaps because the PCB leaders had direct access to Elza, while Prestes tried to follow the situation from a distance, tensions between the two centers soon emerge, as the letters indicate. The PCB, especially Martins, adopts a more nuanced position as February goes along, tempered by doubts, while in Méier, Prestes insists on a rigidity of conduct that no fact or argument can shake. When— wisely, as history would prove—Martins notes that the "extreme solution" is dangerous, because it might be anticipated and even triggered by the police, and that they could take advantage of Elza's disposal to bring about "a nasty scandal" and "separate us from the masses for some time," Prestes claims to agree with his reasoning but adds that "this is only an extra obstacle we need to overcome." When Tampinha and Martins start to believe that those notes from Miranda, the primary pieces of evidence against the Girl, might actually be from Miranda, Prestes reveals himself to be nothing less than an expert in handwriting analysis, sending them the following list of "evidence" that someone was falsifying the handwriting of the party's secretary-general:

- different slant
- overly imitated details
- italics of *ii* exaggerated
- Capital *G* written two or three ways
- Lowercase *r* obviously forced, because difficult to imitate
- *t* whose writing varies from letter to letter

Finally, on February 18, Martins admits his doubts and dares to propose the suspension, even if temporary, of Elza Fernandes's death sentence, or in his words, "maintaining the status quo":

We think that the writing actually is his (Miranda's). We think that the content displays a state of despair that is unjustified by a leader of his responsibility . . . We also find inexplicable his ease of communication with other prisoners and visits from the Girl, when others who are less important remain strictly incommunicado . . . We have, however, regarding the Girl, gone with maintaining the existing status quo until we can see the situation more clearly and hear your opinion. We believe that, due to the intricacies of the case, maintaining the status quo is advisable . . . We will strengthen surveillance surrounding her awaiting your opinion, which must be final.

Poor Martins. Prestes's rebuke, in a letter dated February 19, is that of a professional revolutionary addressing a pathetic amateur:

I received yesterday's note from Martins, as well as the alleged notes from Miranda. I was painfully surprised to see your lack of resolve, because I assume Martins had written on behalf of the National Secretariat, which had just gathered.

Comrades, one cannot direct the party of the proletariat, the consistently revolutionary class, in this way.

Even without being familiar with the originals of the alleged notes from Miranda, already in a letter from yesterday, I had formulated my opinion regarding what we needed to do. But supposing that the notes really are in

Miranda's own handwriting (I am convinced otherwise, as I shall explain below), how do you reach your conclusions? Why adjust the decision about the Girl? What does one thing have to do with another? Was there or was there not betrayal on her part? Is she or is she not extremely dangerous to the party, entirely at the service of the enemy, knowledgeable of many things, and sole witness against a large number of comrades and sympathizers?

On the other hand, if you believe the notes are real, how can you qualify this "weakness" of "our comrade Miranda"? Betrayal is betrayal and all the greater the more responsible the traitor is. But let us return to the case of the little girl. Fully aware of my responsibility, I have given my opinion from the very beginning on what do with her . . . That is why I do not understand your wavering. The National Secretariat is sovereign, and its decisions should not "await your opinion, which must be final," as Martins says in his letter. Such language is not worthy of our party leadership, because it is the language of cowards, incapable of a decision, fearful in the face of responsibility. Either you agree with the extreme measures, and in this case they should have already been resolutely implemented, or then disagree and therefore boldly defend your own opinion, not allowing yourselves to be influenced by anyone.

It is impossible to lead without taking on responsibilities. Furthermore, leadership does not have the right to waver on matters that concern the very security of the organization.

You will comprehend the vehemence of what I have written, because it reflects, with the necessary candor between us, all of my sadness given this hesitation from the leadership, who hold the future of the revolution in Brazil in their hands.

On the following day, February 20, Bangu sent Prestes the following reply:

I have just received your letters about the case of the Girl. If we did not immediately put into effect the measures you proposed, it was due to reasons that seemed just to us, that could result in disconnecting the party from the masses. The Girl is being held; therefore, the matter could be resolved calmly and safely. The fact that we are making arrangements with you once more and are asking for a final decision does not mean that, if you were not here, we would not have made a strong decision. But, using all the experience that you have, we want to work out matters by weighing them, since there is still time for this.

Now, do not be concerned that it will not be done properly, as the issue of sentimentality does not exist here. We have put the interests of the party above all else . . .

Continue to write and assist us. But dispose of this poor impression you have of the current leadership, as this is the leadership that has undergone several years of training and development by the party and is willing to carry out your task over all obstacles.

An amalgamation of wounded pride, resentment, and subservience, Bangu's reply made it clear: Prestes's rebuke had sealed Elvira Cupello Calônio's fate.

Maria opened the door without a word and, as was her nature, disappeared. Xerxes was already in his usual spot, in pajamas, his cane resting next to him against one of the arms of his chair. Eyes closed and mouth open, head flung back on the end of his greenish-white neck stretched out like a chicken for slaughter, the old communist appeared to be asleep. Molina stood motionless in the middle of the room for a few moments, trying to figure out if he was still breathing. It was hard to tell. He was just about to yell for Maria when Xerxes moved his head with a groan. Without opening his eyes, in a voice that was barely above a whisper, he said, "The end is near, my boy. It is already here. See?"

Molina didn't answer. The idea that it might not be just another meeting in the infinite series of meetings with Xerxes was sickening—he thought it best not to think about it. He sat down on the couch and, turning on the recorder, pushed it toward the edge of the coffee table, as close as possible to the old man's muted voice. Noise from the street, buses, children playing, and from the building itself—cheesy music on the maid's radio, toilet flushes, the elevator—all mixed together in a nauseating hum.

Without opening his eyes, Xerxes whispered, "Where are we?"

The impression that this question meant more than was apparent—where they were not just at that moment, but in history itself, in the world—sparked uneasiness inside Molina that seemed to swallow up the oxygen around him. Camila was unreachable by phone. She had changed hotels without telling him, and her cell phone was turned off or had no signal. He didn't know where she was. He didn't even know where he was. "The uprising," he replied.

Xerxes finally opened his eyes and stared at him like he didn't understand.

Molina raised his voice, even though he knew the man's problem wasn't his hearing. "The insurrection!"

"Ah," said the old man. "Of course. One day November arrived and, well, it was what you saw. Nothing happened. A handful of people tried to take two or three barracks. The government had been forewarned; they squashed it like someone killing a louse between their fingernails. Snap. Our revolution lasted just a few hours. Nothing happened."

Then, silence. Molina watched Xerxes's eyes, closed once again, then the red light on the recorder, and grew impatient. What was the matter with him? Did he really think that kind of brevity would be sufficient?

"Where were you that night?"

His question was met with a wishy-washy smile. Molina shifted on the couch, anxious. What if Xerxes's fatigue was contagious?

"Riding up and down on the tram," Xerxes said, "like a fool. Trying to understand what was going on. Dying to find a place, just a little place, where there was a struggle going on. I was carrying a cloth bag with me with some heads of cabbage at the top to conceal twenty-five homemade grenades made out of jelly jars. I went through three or four army roadblocks with that bag, sweating bullets, thinking, *This is it.* No one stopped me. Nothing happened."

"What did you do with the grenades?"

"What could I do? I took them home. I gave Gina the cabbage to cook and I hid the bag in the pantry. Later on I buried them in the backyard. But it doesn't matter." The old man shook his head with sudden impatience, his voice suddenly strengthening, "That's not what I mean."

"Then tell me what you do mean, sir."

"Terror, son. Filinto Müller's murderous police force caught everyone in no time. First Berger, the German. He had the saddest ending a person can have. Tortured day after day, hour upon hour, minute upon minute, for years. Until he went totally crazy. Sobral Pinto filed an appeal with the National Security Tribunal to try to save Berger. His appeal, a stroke of genius, was based on the law of animal protection. Because a rabid dog would have been treated more humanely."

"Did it work?"

"Of course it wasn't going to work," Xerxes huffed, sounding more awake. It was clear that part of his prodigious energy, what little he had left, was coming back as he spoke. He reached for the cane next to him and laid it across his knees. "When Berger was released on amnesty, in '45, he was mad as a hatter, a total nutcase. He went back to East Germany to die in hospice. His wife, Elise, who they called Sabo, had already gone, delivered to the Nazis with Olga. This special sadism Vargas's police exercised with Berger was never explained very well. Prestes—Brazilian, a subject of lore, potential martyr—didn't get a scratch. Yes, the German was a Jew, which didn't help him. But sometimes I think the explanation for their having done what they did with Herr Arthur Ewert has more to do with propaganda. And geopolitics. It was as if Brazil was sending a shrill message to the world: just look at what we do to communist foreigners in this country! Are you sure you want to come here to build a revolution, disrupt the surroundings? Are you prepared to contend with us? But that's also not what I want to say." Xerxes looked around as if searching the corners of the room for what he really wanted to say. "I have to be careful, choose my words well, you understand? I didn't think time would be so short. We're never prepared. The end announces itself your whole life, but when it comes . . . Canellas—remember Canellas?"

It occurred to Molina that Xerxes could be delirious. One moment he was talking about downsizing his story to make it fit in the tiny amount of remaining time he imagined he still had, and the next he was going backward in time. It was getting difficult to ignore the signs that this wasn't going be just another in the infinite series of meetings with the old man. From the kitchen came the horrendous noise of a blender and, for half a second, the agonized scream of a dinosaur doodled around in Molina's imagination.

"Time is short," repeated Xerxes. "It's about that typically filial feeling, son. The sickly mixture of resentment and eagerness to please that cripples those who don't feel loved by their father. You know what I'm talking about, right? The PCB, after behaving so badly in its early infancy, never got rid of the Canellas syndrome. Elza died because of this. Because an insecure, cowardly, pathetic son wanted to impress his father. Just for that. There's no such thing as sentimentality here, Bangu says to Prestes. By Rosa Luxemburg! All of a sudden, not being sentimental proving to the man from the International that those petty bourgeois deviations of Canellas's were a thing of the past, this took on such a monstrous importance that all the rest became insignificant. The PCB knew there was no way they'd be able to make a revolution in Brazil, but so what? It had to impress its father. It knew that Elza was innocent, but it had to impress its father. That's what took me so long to understand. That's what I was light-years away from understanding in February of 1936, the hottest February on record for Rio, a perfect hell, when I went door-to-door, asking for Elza. I had heard rumors that she would be put to death, of course. Everyone heard that; even the newspapers speculated. No one seemed to know. Chico Meirelles, the only one who had agreed to house Elza after she was released, told me she had been picked up at his home by members of the leadership and taken to a secure location. Where? Chico didn't know. I went from comrade to comrade, knowing full well I shouldn't be doing that, that by making so many waves I was violating a golden rule of the party. I didn't care; it didn't matter to me. With Miranda behind bars, I knew Elza had no one else, and my love for her came back stronger than ever; my sense of responsibility was as big as the world. Some said she was hiding out in São Paulo, others said Uruguay. They even told me she had been sent to Moscow. Before long, everyone was running away from me. They surely took my insistence for provocation; they saw me as just another suspicious piece in that nightmare of a puzzle. Who could you trust? That's how conspiracies work, my boy. Any conspiracy under any flag—there comes a time when you no longer know where you're stepping, what is being said with ulterior motives, and what, having been said by you in good faith, could be used against you in the future. In no other circumstances did words offer so much danger—not even in the most neurotic romantic relationships. The dubiety of the conspirators is infinite. Elza was a Shatov, but a much less guilty Shatov than Shatov, and there was no Virginsky to challenge her sentence in the final minute. I am speaking of Dostoyevsky, of course. I am speaking of *Demons*. I haven't gone completely crazy yet. No one has ever written as well as the old Russian reactionary about the swamp of mistrust into which conspirators inevitably sink. Hatreds sprouted up from day to night where, many times, there had been the most genuine brotherly love."

Molina saw tears on Xerxes's face. It was the first time the old man had cried in front of him.

"Dammit, son," he said, "it's so easy to kill someone in the underground! Killing a person who is part of society, no matter how much of a recluse or loner they may be, is one thing. Letters pile up by the door, food in the pantry spoils—it's a problem. Not someone in hiding; they're the perfect victims. They're already half-dead, walking dead. When someone decides to really kill them, they're halfway there. That's what happened in February, and suddenly it was too late."

On the diffuse edge of his visual field, Molina sensed, but couldn't quite see, the apparition of a new face in the door to the hallway. It wasn't Katharina or Maria; it was a male face. Xerxes, his eyes sweeping the ceiling and hands clenched on the arms of his chair, projected his voice to a high-pitched volume that made the memory of the whisper minutes earlier sound like a paradox.

"Too late," he repeated. "Very early was too late. Elza is the heroine that never was, the antiheroine that never was. Do you understand? A character without a narrative, a grotesquely shaped piece. It is impossible to fit Elza onto any board: neither right nor left, up nor down. She wasn't meant to be there. All that is left of Elza is regret, like an accident. It's uncomfortable, something left over, embarrassingly, after we subtract the revolution from the backwardness, multiply by a mass of dunces, and raise it all to the demagogic power. Condemned to live off sexual and emotional favors for her powerful protector, Elza was a ridiculous girl, poor thing. She adhered to the path of so many playmates from fairy tales, but only to a point, because soon she hit the wall of something she couldn't comprehend. Her death offers no possibility of redemption; it's a vile death. Elza died like a little bitch—by mistake, for sport, out of spite, for nothing. Captain Francisco Davino, in his memoir, anti-communist like every book by former communists, chokes up when he says good-bye to Elza: "Sleep, Elza, your endless slumber; you are avenged." But Davino was wrong. No one avenged Elza. The very idea of avenging her is inconceivable. Avenge her how? Every historical vengeance is an epilogue, a grand finale that forces us to rewrite the previous narrative from this end, transforming injustice into justice, chaos into order. How could they do that with Elza? In what story would she fit? Tell me, what story?"

Molina realized that Xerxes was turning purple. Drool trickled down from the left corner of his mouth, running down his chin and dripping on his chest. Certain the old man was dying before his eyes, he shouted for Maria, for Katharina. Both of them rushed in, followed by a big muscular fellow whom he hadn't met. The apartment in Flamengo had never been so populated. The trio swept Molina to the edge of their whirlwind as six arms juggled yellow injections, colorful pills, and glasses of water—maybe even thimblefuls of vodka, but Molina couldn't be sure. He then saw added to the routine elements of Xerxes's treatment the various contraptions under the arms of the big, strong fellow, all installed in minutes with magical efficiency. He recognized an IV pole, a respirator, a heart monitor. The old man slurred his words, grim and sinister sounding. Holding the recorder that, luckily, he had had the presence of mind to grab from the coffee table before being driven back, Molina started to take off slowly, as if he were trying to hide his escape from himself. Who else was paying attention to him? But as soon as he stepped on the worn tiles of the corridor, he began to run.

Waiting for the elevator was unthinkable. Molina jumped down the stairs like a great liquid mass. In the lobby, facing the sun, he nearly crashed into a pretty older woman who was rushing in the opposite direction, discreet jewels under her red hair, eyes of a familiar green that recently had been crying.

9

Statement from Manoel Severiano Cavalcanti, a.k.a. Gaguinho, on April 29, 1940:

. . . said that the declarant entered the Brazilian Communist Party in the year 1935, via the accused EDUARDO RIBEIRO XAVIER (Xavier), then member of the organization of the Brazilian Communist Party; that later, in the month of December of the same year, he moved from his previous residence at Thomazinho Train Station to the house on Rua Maria Bastos, number 48A, near Camboatá Road, near Deodoro Train Station, but under the local jurisdiction of Ricardo de Albuquerque; that a few days after moving to his new residence, the declarant was called on where he worked, at the quayside, by the accused, EDUARDO RIBEIRO XAVIER, who asked him if he could accommodate in his home another comrade of the Brazilian Communist Party, whom he called "the old man"; that the declarant, in fact, only learned later that the "old man" was the accused, FRANCISCO NATIVIDADE LYRA (Cabeção Lyra); that the declarant acceded and invited EDUARDO RIBEIRO XAVIER to visit him in his new home, supplying him, so that he might do so, with the address and directions for the route he should take to get there; that the declarant also remembers that one Sunday the accused, EDUARDO RIBEIRO XAVIER, appeared at his house and had lunch there with him, and examined the room which was intended for FRANCISCO NATIVIDADE LYRA (Cabeção Lyra); that at this moment the accused, EDUARDO RIBEIRO XAVIER, declared the room suitable, arranging with the declarant to return within two days to accompany the accused, FRANCISCO NATIVIDADE LYRA, to his new home, which he in fact did, the latter taking up residence with the declarant; that around one week after welcoming his new guest, the accused, EDUARDO RIBEIRO XAVIER, returned to the declarant's house, to Rua Maria Bastos, number 48A, accompanied by a skinny girl, fifteen or sixteen years old, who gave the name Elza Fernandes, but that after her murder, he learned from reading the newspapers, which covered her disappearance, that she was Elvira Cupello Calônio; that on this occasion, the accused, EDUARDO RIBEIRO XAVIER, asked the declarant to also house the afore-mentioned minor in his home, under the allegation that she was also a comrade of the Brazilian Communist Party; that after some time she would be sent to São Paulo, to which, the declarant acquiesced; that from the outset Elvira Cupello Calônio (Elza Fernandes) proved to be a good comrade, spending all her time perform-ing household chores for the declarant; that soon after the arrival of Elvira Cupello Calônio (Elza Fernandes), the accused, ADELINO DEYCOLA DOS SANTOS, member of the Brazilian Communist Party, appeared at his house, whom the declarant knew only by the nick-name "Chico," who also stayed at his house, submitting the minor Elvira Cupello Calônio (Elza Fernandes) to long interrogations, beginning on the first day; that the declarant did not attend the aforementioned interroga-tions, but he was made aware of them each day when he returned from work around six thirty in the evening, via FRANCISCO NATIVIDADE LYRA, who then told him everything, using roughly the following expressions: "Chico, with pen and paper in hand, really pinned the girl today, and the little comrade was pressed on some question"; that this continued to take place until one day in the month of January, or beginning of February [Gaguinho brings the date forward by one month], of the year 1936, when the accused, HONÓRIO DE FREITAS GUIMARÃES, who the declarant knew by the name Martins, and EDUARDO RIBEIRO XAVIER (Xavier) appeared at the home of the declarant; that on that day were gathered the accused, HONÓRIO DE FREITAS GUIMARÃES (Martins), ADELINO DEYCOLA DOS SANTOS (Chico), EDUARDO RIBEIRO XAVIER (Xavier), FRANCISCO NATIVIDADE LYRA (Cabeção Lyra), and the declarant, who, incidentally, was left out; that after the meeting the accused, HONÓRIO DE FREITAS GUIMARÃES (Martins), called the declarant onto the porch facing the backyard, informing him that Elvira Cupello Calônio (Elza Fernandes) would no lon-ger be traveling to São Paulo because, as a traitor of the Brazilian Communist Party, she should be murdered; that the declarant hesitated but later acceded when the accused, HONÓRIO DE FREITAS GUIMARÃES (Martins), stated that it was an act of great responsibility, that which they had prepared and were going to perform, with the collaboration of the declarant; that, when coffee was made, the victim brought a cup to the accused, HONÓRIO DE FREITAS GUIMARÃES, who was found seated in the next room, and prepared to sit beside him; that at that moment, treacherously, the accused, FRANCISCO NATIVIDADE LYRA (Cabeção Lyra), coming from the backyard holding a rope, joined the declarant and the accused, ADELINO DEYCOLA DOS SANTOS (Chico), and EDUARDO RIBEIRO XAVIER (Xavier), entering unexpectedly in that part of the house; that at the moment the victim, as the declarant mentioned above, went to sit down, the accused, FRANCISCO NATIVIDADE LYRA (Cabeção Lyra), quickly approached said minor, wrapping the rope around her neck, and gave a violent tug, resulting in her attempting to fight back; that at this moment, all of the accused parties were involved in the act of strangulation, at the command of the accused, HONÓRIO DE FREITAS GUIMARÃES (Martins), saying they should all help eliminate the "villain"; that thereby said minor was thrown to the ground, with all parties participating in the strangulation; however, he is unable to specify who tightened the rope and who held down the victim, insisting nevertheless in stating that all the aforementioned accused parties, including the declarant, took part in the execution and the consummation of the crime; that the declarant is therefore sure that the accused, HONÓRIO DE FREITAS GUIMARÃES, took part in all acts of the crime and did not remove himself from the site, as an example to the others; that he also does not remember having seen the accused,

EDUARDO RIBEIRO XAVIER, being involved in any fainting fit and does not believe such a thing happened, due to the spirit of the decision with which all the accused reported the murder of Elvira Cupello Calônio after the interview he had had with Martins, as well as the calm and precision with which all parties committed the crime; that when Elvira Cupello Calônio was dead, the accused, HONÓRIO DE FREITAS GUIMARÃES (Martins), gave a short speech to those present, saying at the end that they had just eliminated a villain . . .

With a ceiling so high it became lost in darkness, the vast reading room in the National Library, lined with anti-quated microfiche readers, had a grandeur that contrasted absurdly with the modesty of the facilities, like a little favela slapped up inside a cathedral: rickety chairs, exposed wires, flickering lights. The only thing breaking the silence was the squeaking cranks palmed by four or five pale researchers unrolling microfilm strips in their glow of amber light. Blurrily parading before them were dead words, dead ideas, dead passions.

Dead people.

Molina felt his body being wrapped slowly, starting from his feet and rising upward, in a film of cold sweat. He had gone back to Xerxes's apartment that morning, but there was no one home. The short, unfriendly doorman with a harelip, someone he'd never felt the need to exchange more than a curt "good afternoon" with on his previous visits, didn't know and didn't want to tell Molina any more than this: no one was home.

"Heisenberg's uncertainty principle." The words appeared on the screen, pulled from an old piece of economic
news involving the bankruptcy of a multinational company
called Heisenberg Inc. That tapped into something Molina
had read as a teenager, back when esoteric matters of physics made his hair stand on end. The young German physicist Werner Karl Heisenberg had stated the inescapable
indeterminacy of any observation in the realm of subatomic
particles. He discovered that measurement adulterated
an observed phenomenon, making it impossible to gauge
both the velocity and position of a particle. When trying
to set the position, its velocity is affected. It was 1927 when
Heisenberg formulated his principle—Elza was eight—and
its impact on philosophy, art, the very air of the following
decades, Molina believed, was so decisive that it was exempt
from any commentary. That may not even be true, but for
him Heisenberg's principle was poetry, not physics, and for-
going any comments helped him to not overthink it. Even
so, he knew Einstein had never liked that story of uncertainty—though he had been the first to point out the path
that would lead there—and even invoked God against it,
saying He doesn't play dice. But in the National Library
that afternoon, Heisenberg was at best a close metaphor to
what Molina was feeling, breathing deeply to try to stem the
course threatening to transform the building in Cinelândia
into an ocean liner on rough seas. It seemed reasonable to
assume that, when the physicist wasn't looking, elementary
particles went back to behaving themselves with the primor-
dial purity that characterized them since the beginning of
time. If purity couldn't be observed, there was the consola-
tion of knowing it was there. But did an equivalent of that

dry land—inaccessible but firm—exist in the story Xerxes had told him?

Depending on the point of view, a point of view nearly always chosen the day before, Elza was a nasty piece of work, or she was the innocent victim of a cowardly massacre. Miranda was the national communist militancy's larger-than-life talent with a silver tongue, or the most perfidious traitor of the revolutionary cause to ever spring up on Brazilian soil. Prestes, a legend, the greatest hero of the left in the Americas, or a charismatic leader who missed the boat and was swallowed up by his own delusions of grandeur. It was of little help to think they could be all those things, or a bit of everything, in a sort of kaleidoscope. There was nothing more human than that. The current of relativism that tried to pull along Molina that afternoon in the National Library was disgusting, slimy. It wanted to transform decades of ideological clashes, sacrifices, suffering, heroism, exile, loyalty, betrayal, courage, horror, decades of life and death, the very substance of the twentieth century, into mushy comedic fodder.

By early evening he was having after-library beers at Amarelinho, feeling like a castaway, the city around him an ocean behind closed doors, when his cell phone rang. His heart racing, he was so sure the call was from Camila that he didn't even check the number on the display before answering. It was Zé. Sounding insistent, his friend invited him to Serafim. The trace of desperation in Zé's voice led Molina to imagine it must be some family hassle, a fight with Tiz, a boring rant. Molina said okay, see you in thirty minutes. He paid his tab and walked toward the bar in Laranjeiras. Half an hour would be just enough time to get there, he calculated, relieved to have a course.

On the corner of Rua da Glória with the short slope that rises from Avenida Augusto Severo, in front of Praça Paris, he met Elza. The same mournful eyes from her lone photograph, the same short hair, the same pert little body, and the same brown skin. The same sixteen years. Just the low-cut shorts and skimpy tank top were inconsistent, signs of a seedy time the little girl from Sorocaba never could have imagined.

"Hey, baby," she said to Molina. "The full package is a hundred, you pay for the room."

Uttered in a tone that somehow managed to mix seduction and indifference, the words didn't make sense to him. What was Elza saying? Where was her yokel accent? Why didn't she sound like a bumpkin from down home in Sorocaba?

Standing in front of the girl, Molina stammered, "What's your name?"

"Tabitha."

"Like Samantha's daughter?"

The laughter of the other transvestites shook him from his trance.

"Ooh," someone shouted in falsetto, "the guy's in love!"

Dizzy, Molina could feel his face burning red. He tried to get away as fast as he could from the group standing on the corner. He was still able to hear Tabitha spit out after him.

"Faggot."

Serafim was packed. At the next table, four guys angrily debated the city's, and the entire country's, hot topic: the torture and murder of three boys from Morro da Providência by thugs from a rival favela, Morro da Mineira. It would have been commonplace, an everyday occurrence, if the victims hadn't been *gifted* to their executioners by a group of army soldiers under a lieutenant's command. Brazilian lieutenants' behavior had changed a lot. Half of the table seemed to find it perfectly reasonable. To the other half, it was the end of the world. They were bellowing so loudly Zé had to nearly shout.

"Everything all right with Camila?"

He was always asking those god-awful questions.

"She's away traveling, but everything's fine. Why?"

"No reason."

"No reason, my ass, Zé."

"No, it's nothing, really."

"C'mon, Zé, tell me why you asked me if everything's all right with Camila."

"Molina, look, it might be nothing."

"What might be nothing?"

"Tiz dreamt that Camila died. It was a very real dream."

"What are you talking about?"

"Last night. She made me promise I'd tell you as soon as possible. Tiz thinks Camila might be in danger."

Molina started to laugh with a mixture of relief and derision. "Are you serious, Zé? Tiz had a dream?" He always thought there had to be something wrong with a woman named Beatriz who instead of going by Bia had turned into a Tiz.

"Look, this wasn't just any dream," said Zé. "Tiz woke up freaking out. It was very real; it really got to her. Tiz has this thing. I didn't believe it either in the beginning, but hey, there's some stuff in her dreams that's spot-on."

When he heard the hello on the other end of the line, Molina was sure Camila had returned. He had spent another sleep-less night, divided between episodes of *The Twilight Zone* and tossing and turning in bed, thinking about the lieuten-ant from Morro da Providência, Xerxes, Elza, his faraway girlfriend. At some point in the middle of the night, those disconnected ideas had formed meaningful relationships, which now he was unable to fully reconstruct.

"Camila!" he shouted into the phone.

The laughter that came over the line was sexy and humiliating. "This is Luz, Mo."

He bit his lower lip until it was sore. That's what he got for calling when he was still asleep, before breakfast. But, after the initial callousness, the teenager had good news for him.

"Camila gets back today," she said. "Pretty soon actually. Why don't you come over and wait for her?"

He went. A half hour later they were alone in the apart-ment on Rua do Russel, Luz in her bedroom, Molina in the living room with a book on his lap: *Stalin's Folly*, by Constantine Pleshakov. The author explained how the Soviet dictator, after years of courting his German coun-terpart, was suddenly paralyzed when Hitler, unyielding in his determination to treat communism as an enemy of the Third Reich, invaded the Soviet Union. Checking his watch the whole time, Molina was so distracted he could barely read. At one point, not much before lunchtime, Luz came out in bare feet and sat next to him on the couch.

"Am I bothering you?"

She was wearing a pair of tight denim shorts and a yellow Hello Kitty T-shirt cut with scissors along the hem. Molina willfully averted his eyes from Luz's tanned stomach, with its silver belly-button piercing, the downy shadow between her navel and the button of her shorts seeming to point the way. Forcing his gaze upward, he noticed something that had escaped him minutes earlier when he arrived: the girl had swapped her usual green streak for a bolder two-tone pattern in turquoise blue and pumpkin orange.

"Of course not," he replied.

"You read too much, Mo."

He smiled. What could he say? He'd never seen Luz reading anything other than the worksheets she pored over for her homework, always with headphones in her ears. She didn't even touch the celebrity magazines her mom collected. In the nearly one year the residents of that house had been in his life, Molina had switched from contempt to a certain respect for this personality trait in Luz. She nurtured a powerful indifference for anything that existed in the world before her. It wasn't quite a form of selfishness, or maybe it was more than that. Luz dwelled in her own present—her body, her extreme youth—with glorious unawareness. If she were a philosopher, she would be an idealist: the world only existed insofar as she, witnessing it, gave it existence. All she had to do was turn around and *let there be light*. Pre-Luz: here was only chaos, the indeterminate, darkness. Not that she completely ignored important milestones, dates, names, those kinds of antiquated relics from the classroom. She was smart enough to memorize and repeat those subjects more or less adequately. Molina suspected they didn't make a lot of sense to her, but he also knew it had been years since a person had needed to grasp any meaning to make it through the school system.

It was when the subject landed on widely circulated cultural items that the girl really stood out. Like the

Beatles—the example he deemed most impressive. Or the pyramids in Egypt, the hippie movement, the Route of Santiago de Compostela, Lampião and Maria Bonita, Charlie Brown, Marilyn Monroe, Hitchcock, Hiroshima, the pope, Tom Jobim. It was in these moments of mundane trivia that Luz's ignorance, like a male peacock's tail in full mating dance, flared in all its splendor. She knew nothing about these things. She didn't want to know. She made a point of not knowing and, more than that—and where Molina managed to catch a glimpse of genius in the ignorance of Luz and her generation—she was extremely proud of not knowing, holding the banner of her idiocy up high. Apart from that, she was a cool girl.

Out of the blue, like someone commenting that it's going to rain, Luz said, "You know Camila's traveling with a guy, don't you? Some dude named Franco?"

"What?"

Luz nodded bleakly. "You didn't know . . ."

Molina felt himself sinking into the couch. Franco?

She smiled scornfully. How could such a young girl smile so scornfully?

"*Franco* Franco?"

"Sorry to break the news to you like that, Mo."

Molina started to turn from pale to purple. "Are you serious?"

He buried his head in his hands, his fingers crawling along his forehead like a plowshare. Feeling Luz stroke his hair, he still didn't completely believe it. Camila, a *slut*? A professional liar? It dawned on him that his doubt was a form of defense, a natural anesthetic secreted by the body in situations of acute pain. It was all quite clear now. What an idiot he had been. It made perfect sense—her sick admiration for Cobra. That bitch!

"Mo."

"Luz, I don't want to hear any more."

"I like you, Mo. It sucks to see you being made a buffoon."

"Thanks. Now be quiet and let me think."

"Think about what?"

"What I'm going to do with your sister's neck."

"You're not going to do anything."

That hurt him. "Of course I am," he protested.

"No, you won't. Not to her. You're too much of a nice guy to do that. You can get all macho and leave, ditch the slut, and go heal your jealous wounds with other sluts. You might do that, but that's it."

For a split second Molina had the impression Luz was enjoying herself more than ever. Suddenly he croaked, "What's going to happen to me?"

The girl stared at him sadly, a faded smile on her lips. "You're a loser, Molina. A big ol' loser. You must be good in bed or else my sister wouldn't be with you, 'cause she's a total nympho, she couldn't take it. But a loser who's good in bed is still a loser."

His eyes welled up. As if confirming the teenager's diagnosis, he murmured, "Ah, Camila."

"Give me a break," she said, jumping up from the couch and disappearing into the depths of the apartment.

He sat staring at the dark screen of the giant TV that overpowered the room. Slowly, images of Camila engaged in elaborate sexual positions with Franco began to appear on the black surface. *His, his, his?* He cried a little, stopped crying, cried some more. Soon he realized the scenes in the little porn film had begun to repeat. His state of imaginative abjection demanded more information, dates, details. He stood up and strode firmly to Luz's room.

The door was ajar. He pushed it.

Standing in the middle of the room, hands on hips, the teenager stared at him from under the shock of blue-and-orange hair. There were clothes piled next to her bare feet: a little ball of yellow fabric, a blue spot of denim. The clothes she was wearing earlier.

"What took you so long?"

He walked to her and they fell onto the unmade bed.

Soon afterward, he fell asleep, passed out in the embrace of his ex-girlfriend's sister. He awoke to hysterical shrieking, shrieking from out of a horror movie. Even before he turned over and saw Laura standing in the bedroom door, Molina already knew he was a goner.

10

——

In the book Prestes: lutas e autocríticas, *based on a long inter-view Prestes gave journalists Dênis de Moraes and Francisco Viana in 1982, the Knight of Hope claimed that he did not order Elza's murder:*

> What happened was the police linked her death to a letter from me, written before my arrest, in which I recommended punishment for traitors. It was the party that ordered Elza's death.

Up until his death in 1990, Prestes denied his involvement in the murder of Elvira Cupello Calônio. But, even among staunch leftist ranks, it is difficult to find a serious historian today who will deny the evidence contained in those letters from 1936. The most you might find is a rationalization of the mitigating circum-stances of realpolitik, "war is war," nothing less than the old raison d'Etat. No different than the Vargas government would invoke to justify its own crimes, just viewed upside down through the lens of the insurrection. As Anita Leocádia Prestes told me in an interview via e-mail:

Said execution was undertaken by the PCB in a political climate that was considered a revolutionary war. In war, the enemy or the traitor must be treated as such. In this case, the information that was available to the leaders of the PCB was that Elvira Cupello was working for the police, denouncing comrades. If there was any error, it was due to the greater error of a false assessment of the political situation at that time.

That there was an error—and a grave error—in the case of Elza Fernandes is something no one argues today. Prestes himself highlights this in his 1982 interview. He explains to the journalists how the events of 1935 scarred the movement, not only because of the arrests but because of how the circumstances paved the way for errors the party would continue to commit into the early '40s. Prestes does concede that Elza's execution was one of the "most negative swings" for the party at the time, referring to her as a "useful innocent." He reminds the journalists that she had no political training or basic education to speak of, and as a result she didn't realize how she was being used by the police, being followed to homes where comrades were later arrested. She was a liability. Prestes makes a point to explain how the person who killed her later killed himself, feeling more like he'd committed a crime, not a just act for the betterment of justice.

If Prestes's insistence on absolving himself from blame is unwavering, the reference to the series of arrests in the wake of Elza's visits and the mention of her killer's suicide introduce new elements of confusion. As soon as she got out of jail, Elvira went to Copacabana, following Miranda's instructions, and knocked on the door of a sympathizing physician. This created something of a headache for Dr. Barbosa de Mello, who promptly turned away the Girl, but he was not arrested. As for the suicide, Prestes seems to be mixing the case of the Girl with that of Tobias Warschawski, a student executed in 1934. One of Warschawski's alleged killers turned up dead some time later, in an apparent case of suicide. Despite these inaccuracies, the rest of Prestes's interview is sufficient to make it clear that in his opinion, albeit a few decades too late, Elza was acquitted of the charge on which she was killed.

Combined with what we know from other sources, it is legitimate to infer that Prestes regretted that letter from February 19, the stern father's scolding that determined the Girl's fate. However, after acknowledging the error of the decision to execute Elvira, the question of its perpetrator remains, and he never admitted this. He even gives an imaginary version of the trial that convicted him as instigator of the crime. He claims that Sobral Pinto assured Prestes that he would be acquitted, though the others wouldn't be. Prestes says he refused to accept this and found inspiration in the day's date: November 7, 1940, the Gregorian-calendar anniversary of the Russian Revolution. The party leadership had fallen, and as Prestes recalls it, standing before Judge Mayard, he pledged allegiance to the party, citing the auspicious anniversary. Mayard saw no relevance in Prestes's declaration, but Prestes insisted that the date was of universal importance to all of mankind. Then, according to Prestes, Raquel Gertel, who was at the trial, shouted "Viva Prestes!" The police stormed in and arrested her. Prestes claimed the racket made the judge turn acquittal into conviction at the last minute, sentencing him to thirty years. As Prestes sees it, he deserved to be acquitted because, in his words, "I had nothing to do with the crime. It was Honório who confessed, along with other party members."

In his book Combate nas trevas (Fighting in the Darkness), *communist historian Jacob Gorender criticizes Prestes for what he calls "pseudo-self-criticism." Gorender states the obvious: nothing in that conviction from 1940 corroborates the theory of a delayed metamorphosis from acquittal to conviction. He adds that the discourse of the Comintern envoy at the National Security Tribunal "had a diversionary purpose: Prestes wanted to avoid a clear stance on his participation in the murder of Elza Fernandes." From an analysis of the correspondence from February 1936, Gorender considers this participation to be proven beyond any doubt. The letter in which Prestes fancied himself a handwriting expert in order to support Miranda's innocence—and, therefore, Elza's guilt—leads the historian to characterize Prestes as egregiously flippant in how he demeans a comrade by acting as an expert on a matter he had no firsthand knowledge of, ignoring the opinions of fellow party members. Gorender equates Prestes's behavior to that of a mythological figure's ego, so set in his beliefs that he ignores what new information might come to light, especially if it contradicts what he already believes to be true. Gorender has no sympathy for Prestes and goes so far as to call him a liar for shirking responsibility for Elza's death. He writes, "At that extremely delicate moment, a minimum amount of sensitivity on his part would have been sufficient to save the life of an innocent comrade and avoid the 'brutal crime.' Instead, he pushed Elza Fernandes to her death by strangulation."*

Marly Vianna, who recorded thirty hours of interviews with the old leader for her book, told me she twice attempted to get him to talk about the sensitive subject: "What about Elza?" Both times Prestes dodged the question: "No, that was another thing, that was another thing," he would say, as if engaged in another line of thought at that moment and postponing the conversation for a more convenient time. "That was the only thing he never wanted to discuss," says Marly, who understood the hint and didn't bring it up again.

The phone rang at midmorning. It never rang, but it was ringing. Wrong number, for sure. Or a telemarketer. It kept ringing as Molina painfully emerged from the abyss and reached out to answer it.

"Luxemburgo Holdings, one moment, please."

What do you mean, one moment, please? You called me, you moron! That's what Molina would have shouted at the girl, if shouting like that wouldn't have been so much work, and if the voice were still there. But it was already gone, replaced with a vaguely familiar player-piano jingle. *It's amazing how in this country everyone whose job it is to talk on the phone, from the northernmost corner of Roraima to the southeastern border, speaks with a São Paulo accent,* Molina thought, vaguely surprised to see his apathy hadn't completely blunted his critical spirit.

Then, with a jolt, he identified the melody.

At first he thought it was an auditory illusion, but he concentrated on the bars that followed, erasing all doubt: in a music-box version, *pling pling plong,* he was hearing none other than "Bella Ciao," the old Italian communist song Xerxes had taught him:

Una mattina mi son svegliato,
o bella, ciao! Bella, ciao! Bella, ciao, ciao, ciao!
Una mattina mi son svegliato,
e ho trovato l'invasor.

Something undefined was awakened within Molina. The voice returned, even more singsong: "Thank you for holding. Could I please speak with Mr. Molina?"

"Yes."

"Am I speaking with Mr. Molina?"

"Yes."

"One moment, please, while I connect you to Ms. Rosa de Torrelodones."

"Who?"

"One moment, please."

Molina already knew Xerxes's name wasn't Xerxes. It was incredible that Molina, a journalist, hadn't sniffed that out in the first week of interviews with the old man, especially after he'd Googled the name along with various references to the story he was telling and the search pulled up nothing. At the time Molina didn't think it was a problem, at least nothing urgent. Xerxes was Xerxes, just like Elza was Elza, Miranda was Miranda, Gruber was Gruber. Given the circumstances, what good was a mere birth certificate?

Besides, he thought he'd have all the time in the world to handle the bureaucratic details of this book. The idea of disturbing Xerxes's stream of nostalgia with vital records fiddle-faddle seemed to him of unforgivably bad taste. This was the old man who refused to die, cane in hand and stormy look in his eye—pyramid, hieroglyph.

But now, stumped on an incomplete story that refused to make sense and without a verified first or last name to work with, what Molina found unforgivable was that very lapse, definitive proof of his incompetence and penchant for inaction, his extraordinary talent for leading himself down dead-end roads. *The world is but the product of the mind that dialogues with itself.* These words had begun to haunt his sleepless nights without him knowing where they came from. Was it Rod Serling? He remembered what Camila used to say about his passion for *The Twilight Zone*: only an eternal teenager could be so impressed by those little stories filmed before he was born, the sudden plot twist, and the euphoria of the aha moment when all was explained. That was it. What? Night after night, Camila's absence throbbing like a physical pain, he awoke, panting, from a dream in which there was a mask under another mask under another mask ad infinitum, leading him to those words that stalked him from the depths of his subconscious like a caption that explained nothing: *The world is but the product of the mind that dialogues with itself.* He eventually got used to it, to the humor he suspected wasn't its author's intention, though that was the best part—the mind that dialogues with itself even when it runs out of things to talk about. *Will it rain? I don't think so. Perhaps early in the morning. Maybe, maybe.*

By his tenth visit, the doorman with the harelip lost his temper with Molina. "Nobody home," he would say in the beginning, "apartment's locked up." One day he changed his story: "They've already been by to get the furniture, a truck was here," and he seemed happy to be trampling Molina's hopes. In any event, Molina wasn't going to give up so easily. He needed to reconnect with Xerxes, so he continued to show up at the building in Flamengo every other day.

"Are you sure no one has left a letter for me? A note?"

That was when the doorman lost his composure completely and threatened to call the police. Molina burst into a fit of laughter. "You can call Filinto Müller if you want," he shouted hysterically. "You can have Romano come torture me with needles!"

The man seemed genuinely frightened. "Sir, you're crazy, sir," he sputtered. "This is a family building. Please, leave us alone!"

Sometimes time thins. Other times, it coagulates. That definitely was Rod Serling, but which *Twilight Zone* episode was it, when that radio voice—a voice from another time, said those words? He watched one DVD after another, looking for the answer. Days, weeks, months spent searching. Time was becoming thinner. His days were filled with Xerxes's voice coming out of the computer from one of the twenty-five files that comprised ninety-seven hours of recordings. Sometimes, tired of the blank screen, Molina would write down a small excerpt of what the old man was saying, but the idea of transcribing all that, of digging through the mountain with his little plastic sand shovel, made him want to die. One day he couldn't stand listening to Xerxes talk anymore, and from then on the apartment sat in silence, or as close to it as you can get a few yards away from the billions of buses on Botafogo Beach.

Leaving his apartment catacomb less and less, a thin, bearded Molina waited for time to collapse again. Days, weeks, months. Years? Decades?

Then one day it happened.

"One moment, please."

The last name was Torrelodones. There was an address too, at Rua São Clemente. Everything about it was conspiring to make him push forward.

The Luxemburgo Holdings headquarters was fancier than Molina expected. He didn't know what he'd expected, but it certainly wasn't anything as aristocratic as the mansion to the rear of a large, leafy, humid garden, studded with fountains and stone benches streaked with mud. With its classic clichés—a spitting lion here, a nude Venus with her jug over there, a little boy peeing over in the corner—the fountains turned the shaded garden, just a few yards away from a bustling, clogged, hellish urban artery, into such a peaceful environment that Molina very nearly indulged the desire to lie down on one of the benches and stay there forever, like a slug or hairy caterpillar, forgetting himself in a bubble of silence that the noise of running water made even more silent. The desire was so strong, it could have only sprung from a secret wellspring of early childhood memory. Who would have taken him for a walk in his stroller in a garden like the one at Luxemburgo Holdings?

It was easy to penetrate the mansion's white facade, up four broad marble steps and through a solid wooden door. Molina's presence recognized by omnipresent cameras, he watched as the door opened with a clack before he could even ring the bell. Upon entering, however, he realized the facade was just a shell. Inside was another structure, all in glass, with a revolving door and security guards in suits, like at a bank. It was impossible to tell how many pairs of eyes were fixed on him at that moment. He controlled his impulse to turn around and run away. In any event, it was too late: the wooden door had already shut behind him.

Passing through the glass turnstile, he waited for the door to lock behind him and trap him like a lab rat. He felt an absurd sense of surprise, almost giddiness, when he saw he was on the other side of the air-conditioned cage. The ceiling rose to dizzying heights, a violet light floated in the empty room, and new age music—something that in the '80s it would have been trendy to call "atmosphere"— played softly from hidden speakers. Molina's eyes were slow to find any life in the lobby other than the two security guards in suits flanking the revolving door, who were so ridiculously rigid they didn't look human.

About ten paces in front of him, a distance made longer by the plush carpet, he saw two LCD monitors protruding from a granite counter. Barely visible behind them were two Barbie dolls wearing heavy makeup, the same hairstyles and same clothes. The receptionists at Luxemburgo Holdings were identical twins.

When Molina identified himself, the Barbie on the left motioned to one of the men in suits, who came over and, in a polite voice that didn't match his ugly bison head, said, "Please follow me, sir." A short elevator ride later, the security guard left him in a large office divided into two areas—a desk on one side, seating area on the other, luxuriously bound books behind glass-fronted bookcases, works of art scattered along the walls and floor. Molina was no expert, but he could swear that the rock with a hole in the middle of it to his right was an authentic Henry Moore.

In the seating area to the left, a woman got up to greet him.

Rosa de Torrelodones was the most elegant elderly woman Molina had ever seen. Her hair wasn't red at all, as he'd thought when they first crossed paths at the entrance to Xerxes's building, her eyes moist, him fleeing the scene. It was a pretty blond mixed with gray, the exact color Grace Kelly's hair would be had she ever played a sixty-year-old woman. Impeccably brushed and held back with a white band of fine fabric, her hair framed a well-proportioned face on which only the bare minimum of wrinkles confirmed the age suggested by her general appearance. And those eyes.

At first, Rosa's eyes seemed to be the same green as Xerxes's, but Molina soon realized they were one or two shades on the spectrum closer to blue. Enough that, instead of a liquid substance, as was the case with the old man, they invoked some crystalline ore, the kind that would drive throngs of pioneers to die of malaria ten times over and return from hell to ask for more.

"My name is Rosa de Torrelodones," she said, extending her hand and ushering Molina to the couch. Her voice was her physical elegance perfectly translated into sound. "On behalf of my father, I have a debt with you. He guaranteed you a minimum of three months of work, and it appears I still owe you for one of those. Is that correct?"

Molina nodded yes.

"I apologize for taking all these months to get in touch. Before he died, Daddy made me promise I would seek you out immediately. But the final throes were so drawn out, and so many things were turned upside down in the company. I ended up leaving this"—she coughed—"hmm, experiment of Daddy's for last. I do apologize. I am prepared to add a bonus to your payment as interest and compensation for any discomfort we may have caused you. Naturally, I will ask you to sign a document absolving us of any liability."

Molina raised his finger as if he were ten years old and asking permission from his teacher to speak in class. "Are you Xerxes's daughter?"

Under the circumstances, the woman's smile was even kind, he thought.

"My father's name was Pedro de Torrelodones, dear journalist."

"Writer," said Molina.

"I thought you knew by now. So are we going to have to start from the beginning?"

"That seems appropriate."

"You were deceived," said the woman with surprising brusqueness. "My father involved you in one of his conspiracies, one of his idiosyncratic personal projects—the most idiosyncratic of all. His masterpiece, his final *oohhh!* before leaving the stage."

"That means . . ." Molina started.

"That means my father was never called Xerxes, not even as an alias. None of what he told you happened to him."

Molina felt the lights grow dim, his stomach slowly churning.

"Daddy wanted to tell you everything at the end, come clean, but he didn't have time," the woman continued, but Molina wasn't listening anymore.

He opens his eyes. He is lying on a couch. His shoes have been removed, his collar and belt loosened. He doesn't take long to recognize the sumptuous office of Rosa de Torrelodones, but Xerxes's daughter isn't in sight. There is a younger blond woman tickling his big toes with a long peacock feather. It takes a while for Molina to recognize her. When he saw her the first time, she was wearing a nurse's uniform, not the black dominatrix costume she is wearing now. It is Katharina, without her white clothes, just a few strips of leather barely concealing her spectacularly immense, busty body. Realizing Molina has opened his eyes, she smiles, puts the feather aside, and grabs a whip with a pointed metal tip. He begins to scream.

He opens his eyes. He is lying on the couch. His shoes have been removed, his collar and belt loosened. Katharina has just given him an injection. "Your fever's going down," she says.

When he opened his eyes again, Rosa de Torrelodones was in front of him. Seated on the chair across from him, on the other side of the coffee table, she kept those eyes of hers resting on him as she sipped tea from a china teacup. Another cup and a steaming pot in the same pattern were on the table.

"I owe you another apology," she said. "The way I gave you the news was horribly rude of me."

Embarrassed by his vulnerable position on the couch, Molina sat up. He buttoned his shirt. His clothes were soaking wet. "I don't know what came over me," he stammered. "I think I haven't been eating well."

Rosa filled the second cup and handed it to him. "I'll have them bring in some cookies. Or would you prefer scones?"

"That's fine," he said. He didn't know what scones were, but he'd never had such tasty tea.

"I am sorry if I gave the impression that Daddy had rattled off a string of lies to you, that it was all fake. On the contrary! I may have felt, I will admit, a certain resentment. The way Daddy conducted this project all on his own, dismissing my input; it wasn't like him. That hurt me. We were always so close. Few daughters can be proud of having done for their fathers what I did for Pedro de Torrelodones." After Rosa uttered these words, her eyes took on a glint of defiance that made Molina wonder uneasily what exactly she meant. But he preferred to walk away from that dark edge. The story already had too many bottomless pits. Instead of another free fall, the moment demanded otherwise, that he stand up in outrage and make demands.

"You told me your father didn't experience anything he told me. Now you're telling me nothing was a lie. Which of the two Rosas am I supposed to believe?"

The woman looked at him with a bemused expression. "There's only one Rosa. There were countless Pedros. Did my dad tell you he was an actor when he was younger? Actually, even I'm confused. I have to switch points of view here. Did he tell you his twin brother was an actor? His brother, Pedro?"

"Yes."

"Well, then. He was the actor. His brother Paulo was the man you met all those days. The one who told you the story of Elza and Miranda's ill-fated love, the love triangle whose seeds were sown but that was never consummated. The triangle that loomed there in the air, interrupted just like the revolution. Paulo was the one who told you all that, and nothing, not one thing, was a lie. For Paulo, there was no deeper truth imaginable."

"But Xerxes was Pedro," said Molina.

"Playing the role of Paulo," said Rosa. "Giving a voice to his dead brother. Telling the story Uncle Paulo would have told with the same angry words he would have used, the same urge to bestow justice upon Elza Fernandes, the love of his life, if only life had given him time."

"Your father decided to play God," said Molina, feeling himself teeter between feelings of horror, indignation, and enchantment.

"God? I wouldn't say that. Daddy was an atheist. A playwright, yes, and an actor. Hence the need for an audience. The theater can only exist if that fourth wall looks out on an audience. In this case, you were the audience. I doubt you can even begin to understand the privilege of having been chosen for that role."

Molina placed the cup on the coffee table and raised his hands to his face. He rubbed his eyes with masochistic force.

"Daddy was a great actor," said Rosa. "Pedro Torres. Actors back then had simple names. He thought it better to simplify, shorten Torrelodones. He rehearsed a lot to play Paulo; it was an excruciating process. Daddy's greatest theatrical work without a doubt. Believe me, he became Uncle Paulo. Before he died, he confessed to me that he

181

didn't know to what extent you had fallen for the story. He was always a perfectionist. He couldn't forgive himself for not being able to complete the project. His pride suffered from the holes he had left, the incongruities. 'Bella Ciao,' for example."

"What about 'Bella Ciao'?"

"It's an Italian song from World War II. It couldn't have been sung at a communist gathering in Brás in 1934."

Molina fought the urge to sweep the tea service off the table with his hand. "Was your father even a communist?" he barked.

"Of course." A note of impatience made Rosa de Torrelodones's beautiful voice go slightly out of tune. "A communist until the end. As I said, nothing was a lie. Daddy renounced Integralism when Hitler showed his claws. He entered the party around the time Uncle Paulo left, exactly as he told you. When old Enzo, Gina's father, died, she and my uncle moved to São Paulo. Apparently, her mother had written a tearful letter asking her daughter for forgiveness, saying she needed her company, and off they went. That's how Uncle Paulo approached Sacchetta and wound up falling into disgrace, along with his group, in 1938. Daddy had great esteem for that episode. He suffered greatly in his last days for not being able to stage it for you."

"*The Bowels of Liberty,*" said Molina.

"Right. You know who that great writer was defending, don't you?" Rosa stared at him. "Who was the man who drove out Sacchetta, Uncle Paulo, and the others as Trotskyists?"

"I'm afraid I don't remember right now."

"It was Lauro Reginaldo da Richa, the illustrious Bangu. The fellow who told Prestes there was no sentimentality, that Elza would die, and that was that."

Molina didn't want to give in to the temptation of friendly conversation. He looked around with a sarcastic smile, his arms open, spanning the office, building, and garden. "For a communist, your father sure seems to have been quite the capitalist."

Rather than take offense, as he expected, Rosa nodded in agreement. "Pedro Torrelodones started getting rich in the mid-'70s, as soon as he gave up on the armed struggle. In the beginning, he smuggled Cuban cigars. Then rum and, by extension, vodka, and then everything in between—home appliances, whiskey, jeans. He was fond of saying there were two coexisting worlds living alongside one another, each self-contained, only a translucent membrane separating the two. In any case, I think because of the influence of the Berlin Wall, or maybe the Iron Curtain, we got used to speaking of that border with harsh metaphors of concrete, barbed wire, guards armed to the teeth. Forget all that. Imagine a piece of fabric as delicate as a membrane—not even a membrane, nothing more than an almost immaterial film of molecular resistance, like between water and oil. It seems like nothing but it's enough to keep two universes in their places, each with its own density. That was how Daddy saw the world during the Cold War. One day he discovered that the possibilities offered to someone who could travel from one side to the other, piercing the membrane like passing through a curtain of water, were endless. Once he had learned the trick, mastered the magic, made contacts, he said it was like gaining access to a higher consciousness. Daddy became a demigod. From his new position he saw everything with acute clarity. The dynamics of the circulation of wealth on one side and on the other, like phosphorescent routes in pitch, stress points, the clearest imbalances, places where the membrane was begging, to all laws of physics, to be pierced. I don't know if you understand what I'm talking about. It has nothing to do with politics, ideology. These notions had validity in each of the two worlds of course. A dramatic validity: people killed themselves for them, died for them. But Daddy used to say that as soon as he saw himself in that border zone, what struck him the most was how these things became empty. Like advertising for products taken off the market."

"That's cheap political relativism," snorted Molina.

"Nothing to do with relativism, political or moral. Daddy never said the two sides were equal. I imagine this type of comparison is something that was simply beside the point in his new point of view. The world he described to me when he started grooming me to work with him, at the tail end of the '70s, was more analogous to that of biochemistry, with its exchange of elements that longed, or even more to the point, *had* to pass from one environment to another. It's something totally compatible with the spirit of Marxism, if you think about it. Until the entire world has turned communist, until the class struggle is abolished in all corners of the globe, there would be the need for this exchange. And as each side of the membrane obeyed its own logic, setting its own time, it was a bit like deftly shuffling the past and future, playing with it. Like knowing the name of the horse that will win the race tomorrow. Once you got the hang of it, Daddy used to say it was cowardice. In two years he was rich. In ten, a millionaire. When the Wall came down and everything fell apart, Luxemburgo Holdings was already a long way away from its, shall we say, hidden origins. It had become a completely legitimate business, to use the words of Michael Corleone." Rosa paused briefly and added, with a smile that lasted only for the duration of her words, as if in parentheses, "Daddy adored Michael Corleone." Turning serious again, she continued: "We found out about the brain tumor two years and four months ago. A giant tumor. When the doctors discovered it, it was already the size and shape of a fig. They did everything possible. They opened up Daddy's head to cut out the rot with a knife, dumped radiation on him, gave him enough chemotherapy to kill off a small planet. He nearly died from the treatment, not the cancer. After one year roaming the circles of hell, when Daddy had grown back a few strands of hair and felt like eating and drinking without vomiting up his soul, the exams revealed the tumor had made an even greater recovery. That was when he held my hand and said this little theater performance was all he needed. 'Now it's personal; me against the beast,' he said. He brought together the medical team we had on the payroll, a dozen fools in white, and made a speech. From that day on, Daddy declared the illness the victor. He surrendered himself unconditionally to that magnificent specimen that absorbed the most noxious poisons like it was having a gin and tonic by the pool. So"— and Molina noticed Rosa was now smiling from pure emotion, and upon saying those words the volume of her voice rose slightly—"so Pedro de Torrelodones ordered that all the knowledge accumulated by medicine since Hippocrates would from that moment on be engaged in the mission of letting him live as comfortably as possible with the extraordinary tumor. If the monster gave him debilitating, horrible headaches, he wanted to be medicated with the most powerful opiates and morphine-based painkillers in the world. If it left him dizzy, they were to try to chemically balance him, and if it took away his concentration, they were to focus him. He wanted to attack the symptoms, just the symptoms. He demanded the best palliatives money could buy. As for the rest, he asked that death come when it was time. It would be very welcome."

Molina listened. It occurred to him that he was succumbing to the same sort of spell that had overpowered him in Xerxes's living room—or rather, the living room where Pedro posed as Paulo de Torrelodones. The one that turned him into a hypertrophied hearing aid with some additional secondary organs hanging off it.

"I can imagine what you're thinking," said Rosa, refilling the teacups. "If Daddy hadn't been rich, he wouldn't have been able to take a stand against the medical dictatorship. You're right. It turns out doctors are even more crazy about money than lawyers, so that part was easy. That just left the matter of how to enjoy what time he had left, and sometimes I think the plan sprang precisely from Daddy's greatest fear: fear of the gradual memory loss the doctors predicted. 'Nothing can be done,' those morons said in a little rehearsed chorus. The physical deaths of millions, billions of files stored away, were not open to appeal, as the tumor ate neurons in its war of expansion. Daddy laughed and laughed about that war; he even named his tumor Adolf. Of course, I understood how much his joke was an attempt to hide his fear. Losing his memory seemed worse than death to him, which makes sense. Think about it: at ninety-odd years old, the past is all a person has. What does the future hold? Or even the present? Nothing, of course. Absolutely nothing. There is only the past."

"Dying neurons might be a blessing," Molina caught himself saying, unsure if he was speaking of Xerxes or himself. "I mean, if the guy doesn't want to remember . . ."

"Yes, forgetting can be a blessing," she agreed. "The idea that revisiting our past gives meaning to old age is one of those saccharine Walt Disney notions everyone learned to swallow unquestioningly. Proof, as if any more proof were needed, that stupidity won the war. Because obviously, being what we are, for us human beings it's just a matter of time before a share of our memories take on a putrefied appearance, enough to scare away anyone in their right mind. Even in our dreams there is a substantial region of experienced subject matter that can only be seen through veils of illusion, allusion, metaphor, or metonymy. Therein lies Daddy's genius."

"I'm not following you."

"Daddy didn't know just how deeply Uncle Paulo had really been in love with Elza Fernandes. He believed that romantic evening in the Passeio Público park really had been unforgettable, no question about it. But for Daddy, his brother's infatuation never would have gone beyond a flirtation, a boyish crush, if Elza, instead of dying as she did, had grown slowly older, lost her spice and charm as we all do. But Elza died a child; she was buried like an animal, and my uncle never recovered. Everyone found a way to forget that story. It was a story with no meaning, no moral, no heroism. Even the reactionaries one day grew tired of it. Not Uncle Paulo. Daddy used to say Elza was still alive inside him. She was eating his soul from the inside. For a long time the signs of my uncle's illness never went beyond a marked shift in his personality. He went from being a cheerful and outgoing guy to someone gloomy and dour. He lived with Gina, a wonderful woman, like a grumpy old man lives with a stray puppy. He gave her food, let her sleep inside the house, but the most tenderness he could muster was not kicking the crap out of her. At least that's the family folklore Daddy told me. I myself don't remember Gina very well. I'm too young for that. After she died of appendicitis, in 1954, Uncle Paulo did not wish to remarry. He spoke very little, had no friends. In spite of everything, none of this seemed of great consequence. Many people live that way, grow old that way, half-dead on the inside. Sometimes it takes a hundred years of living like that for a person to die completely. My uncle might still be around today, spoiling everyone's mood with his cantankerousness, had it not been for the incident with Plínio."

Molina noticed the woman's voice lower to a conspiratorial tone.

"Daddy and Uncle Paulo had finally come to a political agreement in the late '60s. With their experience from decades of militancy, they became senior officials in one of the armed organizations that sprung up after the military regime opted for overt fascism, in 1968. I don't know if I should tell you the name of this organization, since it was underground. Of course, all of this is ancient history, but still. Let's call it the Revolutionary Party of the Armed Workers Forefront. What do you say? You accepted Xerxes without hesitation, why not this? One day, for reasons not worth getting into right now, a young member of the organization started behaving erratically. After returning from Cuba, where he had been sent to receive special guerilla training, he started avoiding his comrades, didn't report back on the trip, and when he was approached by one of them he admitted that he was thinking of leaving the movement—which, in his position, and at that time, was an utter impossibility. This young man was called Plínio, and he was executed. Daddy never hid from me that he had participated in the meeting that decided his punishment, and said that his greatest concern was protecting Uncle Paulo. They made up some story that Plínio, after his training in Cuba, was going to grad school in Albania, whatever. If not that, something similar. Anything so long as my uncle didn't find out the truth. Daddy knew his brother's weakness. He knew very well how he viewed vigilantism—any vigilantism—since what had happened to Elza. The problem was that Uncle Paulo found out."

At that point, it seemed to Molina like Rosa de Torrelodones was talking to herself in a sort of trance, her gaze floating adrift in the air of the room.

"Uncle Paulo snapped. *Who decided this? How? When?* He wanted to know everything, every detail, every shred of evidence, the arrangements. Daddy was designated to go see his brother and try to calm him down. That was the stated purpose: to calm him down. In fact, Daddy knew his mission was to assess Uncle Paulo's state of mind, to recommend the next move. Uncle Paulo was in a hideout in Santa Teresa, and one afternoon Daddy showed up without warning. It was on Almirante Alexandrino Street, in a basement. From the entry hall, instead of going up the stairs, you went down. Still, as the building was on the edge of a cliff, the scenery outside the window was, by the vivid description Daddy gave so many years later, truly stunning: half of Rio de Janeiro, the entire bay, just spectacular. Uncle Paulo was standing by the window, absorbed in the view, and he just stood there. Daddy thought he hadn't seen him come in, but suddenly, without turning around, Uncle Paulo said, 'You know what I'm thinking about, Pedro? You can't even see from here all those little men who are putting up that amazing bridge,' and he pointed to the Rio–Niterói Bridge construction site down below, a gently curved line over the steely-gray water. By that time, March 1971, the bridge was already clearly taking shape, a skeleton with no flesh, but the frame was complete, or almost. 'You can't see them, but they say the workers are dying like flies on that project, don't they?' Daddy agreed, encouraging him. Uncle Paulo said, 'It must have been like that at the pyramids in Egypt.' After an almost bucolic pause, standing side by side in silence, two brothers enjoying the beautiful scenery, Uncle Paulo spoke again and calmly said something that sent a chill down Daddy's back. He said, 'But human life means nothing compared to something that big, does it, Brother?' Then Daddy saw there were tears in Uncle Paulo's eyes and tried to give him a hug, but he dodged him violently and began to scream, red with rage, that he was leaving the organization right then, and each remaining minute of his life would be dedicated to writing a book about the story of Elza Fernandes, his first love, his only love, a book so definitive and human and heartbreaking that, after it, no one would ever have the courage to perpetrate a monstrosity like that again."

In the silence that followed, Molina sat listening to Rosa's slightly quickened breathing.

"And then what?" he said.

"Don't ask me to put it into words. It doesn't matter if you are a journalist or a writer. Neither journalists nor writers usually allow for this, but the truth is not everything must be put into words. Then what, you ask? Daddy gave the organization the only report he could. Uncle Paulo had the same fate as his great love."

Like an electric shock in slow motion, a shiver ran up Molina's body, exploding in his head and, as if under a spotlight's glare, revealed the entire mural with dazzling sharpness.

"The book that Uncle Paulo wasn't able to write is your task now," said Rosa de Torrelodones. Standing up, she offered a pink rectangular piece of paper between two fingers. "Here's the check."

Outside, he was startled to see it was not yet dark. Deciding to spend some time in the peaceful garden of Luxemburgo Holdings before plunging back into the chaos on the street, Molina sat down on the first bench he found. An opening for a book came to him:

> *She was sixteen years old. Or so they say. The versions of the story vary. In some, Elza is a grown woman, twenty-one. In most, she's sixteen.*

After studying the words for a few moments, rolling them around from side to side, he concluded that no one would ever get to the end of a book that started like this.

11

————

Letter to Elza that Miranda wrote from prison in mid-February 1936 and signed as Adalba (Adalberto), one of his aliases. It was the letter that led Prestes, Martins, and Bangu to debate graphology. In custody at Gaguinho's house, Elza would never receive it.

Girl:

Why don't you come see me? I waited for you on the day you set. I waited for you on the 10th of February, my birthday, and you didn't come. What happened? I am distressed not hearing from you, and I have no peace of mind. What is wrong, my darling? Tell me.

The enemies are spreading vile rumors about me. I told you to be wary of this, and ordered you to warn our friends. In addition to the physical torture, they are subjecting me to mental torture. If anyone tells you nasty things about me, turn away. The enemy tries to destroy us and break us apart; you need to be very careful with the rumors. Don't give them credence. I am sick; I need money, clothes, and medicine. I trust you and I am waiting for you, and am certain that you will wait for me. My conscience is clear, I stand firm, confident that I behaved like a valiant man, and to the level of confidence my friends always placed in me. May they be careful with the rumors; they are all servicing the enemy. Soon we shall clarify everything. But, Girl, my darling, do not let me go on without hearing from you; it increases my suffering horribly. My heart and nerves are crushed. With your help and comfort, I will certainly survive all of this suffering. Our clothes are definitely lost. Girl, my darling, come console me a little, send word, write me. I await the joyful moment when I will see you again. My darling, help me to fight; I need your comfort. Come, Girl, I am waiting for you. Lots of love, hugs, and kisses from your

Adalba

"Neiva's Coiffeur" said the garish marquee above the entrance. The alley, paved with uneven cement and standing about one and a half meters wide, snaked downhill between two- and three-story buildings, lopsidedly stacked one on top of another, save for the occasional addition jutting out. Surrounded on both sides, the sunlight that did manage to penetrate the alley was residual, like a weak bulb. Molina forced himself to go down, past small porches—which he couldn't tell if they were on the front or back of those houses—little crooked gates, ledges where cats slept on washrags put out to dry. He had the impression that the alley was getting darker and more humid the farther he went, watching the rising numbers: 20, 23, 25. He was looking for 48.

Finding the number on Rua Maria Bastos that corresponded to the house where Elza Fernandes died was, he knew, nothing more than an exercise in journalistic meticulousness. Obviously, the numbers had changed. On the right side of that narrow street in Guadalupe, there were still houses surrounded by some space, grass, a tree or two, but on the left stood a long string of little cottages and modest two-story homes, all crammed against one other to form a single wall that, at one point, opened up like a missing tooth to give way to the narrow alley announced by the sign "Neiva's Coiffeur."

At the bar on the corner they'd told him that number 48 was somewhere down there. Even though Molina had never deluded himself into thinking he would find Gaguinho's suburban house still standing, with its shaded backyard where the body of Elza Fernandes was buried that night in March 1936, he hadn't imagined something so completely different from the original setting as that claustrophobic crevice carved out between shacks, reeking of mildew, fried onions, and wet dog.

It was a dark night and completely desolate. Far away, however, a gigantic coconut palm, the burial's sole observer, phlegmatically swaying its leaves, witnessed the horror.

The maudlin words Captain Francisco Davino dos Santos had written about Elza's burial seemed to come straight out of a fairy tale. Phlegmatic or not, it was hard to imagine a palm tree in this place.

Suddenly, Molina encountered a young boy coming up the hill, four or five years old, his head down, wearing only shorts, followed by a dog with patchy fur. He was the first human being Molina had seen in the alley. It was only then he realized that, in contrast to the actual street above, where a VW van was unloading furniture and trinkets, surrounded by the buzz of a small crowd of onlookers of all ages, the alley was deserted and, stranger still, completely silent. The disconnect between those two vertical stretches full of doors, windows, patios, and ledges, and the almost complete absence of life was absurd. Was he, the outsider, the one responsible for the stillness? He imagined a thousand pairs of eyes following his progress down the alley, peeping at him from behind cracks and curtains. The house numbers were painted crudely by hand next to the doors. Suddenly, he was almost at 60 and was glad to be able to turn back. From that point the slope steepened, turning to stairs ahead, and it seemed to grow even darker. But maybe that was an impression caused by the fear he tried to keep quiet, domesticated, disguised as natural and healthy apprehension, but deep down he knew it to be actual fear.

The risk Molina faced was hardly equal to playing Russian roulette with three bullets in the cylinder. That would not have been the case had he gone a couple of miles farther down the road toward Costa Barros and jumped out of the car to go poking around the Morro do Chapadão slum, leaving his driver, Lulinha, waiting at the wheel. He'd never even heard of Chapadão until Lulinha, chatting away as they flew down Avenida Brasil in his '92 Escort, told horrible stories. But they weren't in Chapadão, a drug-trafficking war zone. They were lower down, a five-minute walk from Guadalupe Mall, a middle-class area by local standards. "A few years ago all this right here was awful," said one of the guys in the bar, "but we cleaned it up." He meant that Rua Maria Bastos now belonged to the territory controlled by the militia. Molina had already suspected that by the looks of the muscular old-timer who sat staring at him from a chair on the sidewalk across the street. Maria

Bastos, a cross street of Pelópidas Passamani, had turned into a sort of closed cul-de-sac, with a black-painted iron gate that was kept open during the day and closed at night. The old-timer was sitting next to the fence, watching everyone coming and going. The street where they killed Elza now had a gatekeeper.

"Don't worry. You can go hunt for that address, no problem," said the only customer in the bar who would open his mouth, but only after Lulinha bought him a beer with Molina's money. Nothing like having a driver with fixer aspirations. Molina was just a pair of ears and was trying to avoid opening his mouth as much as possible so as not to make it any more obvious how much of an outsider he was. The owner of the bar and another guy remained aloof, their lips sealed.

At one point, Molina left Lulinha drinking at the bar and walked out onto the street. He greeted the robust old-timer with a nod that wasn't reciprocated.

"Hello," Molina said. "I was wondering if I might have a word with you, sir?"

The old man made a face as if to say, *Do I have any choice? You're already talking.* Molina could already sense the conversation would get him nowhere but went ahead and asked the man if he knew about a girl named Elza Fernandes being killed on this street.

"I mean way back, in 1936," he hastened to add.

The retired military police officer sat staring at him for a long time, then shook his head slowly but emphatically, and said, as if the mere idea were an insult to his pride as a security guard, "That never happened."

After Molina spun around in the alley, wondering where in the hell number 48 could be—*I guess it doesn't exist; hooray, let's get out of here*—he hastened his step up the hill and, turning a corner, nearly ran into a large dog that was blocking the way. He stopped short, just in time to not hit it. But feeling threatened, the beast got up swiftly and bared its teeth. Molina took two steps back, resisting the urge to rush off down the hill. The dog began to bark loudly and was soon echoed by all the dogs in the neighborhood.

"Sultan!" shouted an old woman.

The dog stopped barking immediately. It ducked its head and slipped through a little iron gate between two low walls. Inside, on a sort of tiny porch, an elderly woman was sitting in a rocking chair, a plaid blanket across her lap. She was half-hidden behind anthuriums and ferns, and he hadn't noticed her just a minute earlier, heading down the hill in search of a mathematical abstraction and fleeting signs of life. Now, however, she dominated the alley with monumental grandeur.

"Come in, son."

He realized disobeying was not an option. Passing through the gate, he suddenly saw, painted on the wall in broad brushstrokes, what by some quirk remained hidden from those walking through the alley. He had found number 48.

Warning

This is a work of fiction based on historical events. Fictional characters, who give their own fictional versions of these events, appear only in the segments in nonitalicized type. The italicized passages that open each chapter are strictly journalistic, based on real documents and interviews, and any use of the first person refers to the author himself.

Bibliography

Amado, Jorge. *O Cavaleiro da Esperança*. 34th ed. Rio de Janeiro: Record, 1987.

———. *Os subterrâneos da liberdade*. 4th ed. São Paulo: Livraria Martins, 1960.

Araújo Neto, Adalberto Coutinho. *Sorocaba operária*. Sorocaba: LINC, 2005.

Barata, Agildo. *Vida de um revolucionário*. Rio de Janeiro: Melso, 1962.

Basbaum, Leôncio. *História sincera da República: de 1930 a 1960*. 4th ed. São Paulo: Alfa-Omega, 1981.

Branco, Carlos Castello. *Retratos e fatos da história recente*. Rio de Janeiro: Revan, 1994.

Caballero, Manuel. *Latin America and the Comintern, 1919–1943*. Cambridge: Cambridge University Press, 2002.

Canale, Dario, José Nilo Tavares, Francisco Viana. *Novembro de 1935: meio século depois*. Petrópolis: Vozes, 1985.

Cavalheiro, Carlos Carvalho. *Salvadora!* Sorocaba: LINC, 2001.

Cobra, Ercília Nogueira, and Adalzira Bittencourt. *Visões do passado, previsões do futuro*. Rio de Janeiro: Tempo Brasileiro, 1996.

Dostoyevsky, Fyodor M. *Obra completa*. Rio de Janeiro: Nova Aguilar, 1995.

Dulles, John W. F. *Brazilian Communism, 1939–1945*. Austin: University of Texas Press, 1983.

Gomes, Ângela de Castro, Dora Rocha Flaksman, and Eduardo Stotz. *Velhos militantes: depoimentos*. Rio de Janeiro: Zahar, 1988.

Gorender, Jacob. *Combate nas trevas*. 5th ed. São Paulo: Ática, 1997.

Joffily, José. *Harry Berger*. Rio de Janeiro: Paz e Terra, 1987.

Karepovsk, Dainis. *Luta subterrânea: o PCB em 1937–1938*. São Paulo: Hucitec/Unesp, 1983.

Krivitsky, W. G. *In Stalin's Secret Service*. New York and London: Harper & Brothers, 1939.

Lacerda, Carlos. *Depoimento*. Rio de Janeiro: Nova Fronteira, 1977.

Lima, Heitor Ferreira. *Caminhos percorridos: memórias de militância*. São Paulo: Brasiliense, 1982.

Malta, Maria Helena. *A Intentona da vovó Mariana*. Rio de Janeiro: Rosa dos Tempos, 1991.

Moraes, Dênis de, and Francisco Viana. *Prestes: lutas e autocríticas*. Petrópolis: Vozes, 1982.

Morais, Fernando. *Olga*. 15th ed. São Paulo: Alfa-Omega, 1989.

Oliveira Filho, Moacyr de. *Um operário no poder*. São Paulo: Alfa-Omega, 1985.

Pandolffi, Dulce. *Camaradas e companheiros: história e memória do PCB*. Rio de Janeiro: Relume Dumará, 1995.

Pereira, Astrojildo. *Construindo o PCB: 1922–1924*. São Paulo: Ciências Humanas, 1980.

Pinheiro, Paulo Sérgio. *Estratégias da ilusão: a revolução mundial e o Brasil, 1922–1935*. São Paulo: Companhia das Letras, 1991.

Pinto, Herondino Pereira. *Nos subterrâneos do Estado Novo*. Rio de Janeiro: Self-published, 1950.

Pleshakov, Constantine. *A loucura de Stalin*. Rio de Janeiro: Difel, 2008.

Prestes, Anita Leocádia. *Luiz Carlos Prestes: patriota, revolucionário, comunista*. São Paulo: Expressão Popular, 2006.

———. *Da insurreição armada (1935) à "União Nacional" (1938–1945)*. São Paulo: Paz e Terra, 2001.

Prestes, Luiz Carlos. *Anos tormentosos: correspondência da prisão, 1936–1945*. Arquivo Público do Estado do Rio de Janeiro, 2000.

Prestes, Maria. *Meu companheiro: 40 anos ao lado de Luiz Carlos Prestes*. 2nd ed. Rio de Janeiro: Rocco, 1993.

Queiroz, Rachel de, and Maria Luiza de Queiroz. *Tantos anos, uma biografia*. São Paulo: Arx, 2004.

Quintella, Ary. *Sobral Pinto: por que defendo os comunistas*. Belo Horizonte: Comunicação, 1979.

Ramos, Graciliano. *Memórias do cárcere*. 15th ed. Rio de Janeiro: Record, 1982.

Santos, Francisco Davino dos. *A marcha vermelha*. São Paulo: Saraiva, 1948.

Sevcenko, Nicolau, ed. *História da vida privada no Brasil*. Vol. 3, *República: da Belle Époque à Era do Rádio*. São Paulo: Companhia das Letras, 1998.

Silva, Hélio. *1935: A revolta vermelha*. Rio de Janeiro: Civilização Brasileira, 1969.

Valtin, Jan. *Do fundo da noite*. Rio de Janeiro: José Olympio, 1942.

Vianna, Marly de Almeida Gomes. *Revolucionários de 1935: sonho e realidade.* São Paulo: Expressão Popular, 2007.

Vinhas, Moisés. *O Partidão: a luta por um partido de massas, 1922–1974.* São Paulo: Hucitec, 1982.

Waack, William. *Camaradas.* São Paulo: Companhia das Letras/Biblioteca do Exército, 1999.

Werneck, Maria. *Sala 4: primeira prisão política feminina.* Rio de Janeiro: Cesac, 1988.

Werneck Sodré, Nelson. *Contribuição à história do PCB.* São Paulo: Global, 1984.

Zicree, Marc Scott. *The Twilight Zone Companion.* New York: Bantam Books, 1982.

About the Author

© Heloisa Fischer

Sérgio Rodrigues was born in the city of Muriaé, in southeastern Brazil, in 1962. He has lived in Rio de Janeiro since 1979. Rodrigues, a driving force in Brazilian journalism, started publishing fiction in 2000 with his short story collection, *The Man Who Killed the Writer*. He is the author of three novels, published in four languages, and the winner of the Prêmio Cultura do Estado do Rio de Janeiro. *Elza: The Girl* is his English debut.

About the Translator

Zoë Perry is a Canadian American translator who grew up in rural southeastern Kentucky. She completed a BA in French and International Studies at Guilford College and an MA in Intercultural Communication at Anglia Ruskin University. Having lived and worked in Brazil for several years, and for briefer periods in Portugal, France, Spain, and Russia, she is currently based in the UK. She has translated work by several contemporary Brazilian authors, including Rodrigo de Souza Leão, Lourenço Mutarelli, João Ximenes Braga, and Paulo Coelho.